Listen To Your Heart

Listen To Your Heart

Fern Michaels

for Erree Enjoy Fern Michaels

Kensington Books
http://www.kensingtonbooks.com

The author wishes to acknowledge the use of the recipes
for corn puppies, shrimp boulettes, and Cajun crab pie
from *Dat Little Cajun Cookbook* by Chef Remy
Laterrade, C.E.C., ISBN 0-9632197-1.
Dat Little Cajun Cookbook Copyright © 1993 by Remy Laterrade
(Relco Ent.: P.O. Box 3943, Lafayette, LA 70502-3942)

KENSINGTON BOOKS are published by

Kensington Publishing Corp.
850 Third Avenue
New York, NY 10022

Library of Congress Card Catalogue Number: 99-68845
ISBN 1-57566-572-7

First Printing: April, 2000
10   9   8   7   6   5   4   3   2   1

Printed in the United States of America

Listen To Your Heart

One

$Gourmet$ $Party$ magazine called the building a picture-perfect Hansel and Gretel cottage, rhapsodizing over the gingerbread trimming, the diamond-shaped windows, and the Dutch doors that looked out onto a miniature front porch, where window boxes chock-full of colorful petunias and geraniums nestled under the gleaming windows. Luscious green ferns on white braided chains hung from the porch ceiling and swayed in whatever breeze found its way to the Garden District. Neighbors and friends referred to the cottage as a cute little converted playhouse, in part owing to the small front porch and the extra room added on to the back. Twin sisters Josie and Kitty Dupré called it their place of business, also known as Dupré Catering. It was all those things by design, a design the twins had come up with to attract new customers. The test kitchen and the working kitchen were set farther back and secluded with the help of well-pruned shrubbery and huge old oak trees that dripped Spanish moss.

Bright red and black stepping-stones in the shape of

ladybugs, a holdover from the twins' childhood years, led customers from the discreet sign at the side of the driveway to the eye-pleasing cottage, where business was conducted six days a week.

Josie Dupré bent down to pick up the eight-pound snow-white Maltese and set her on the corner of the small secretary. "It's just you and me today, Rosie. It's Monday, so things are going to be slow. What that means is, I am going to trim and water all the plants on the porch while you sit and watch me. I'm going to tell you all about my date last night with Mark O'Brien. It's not interesting at all. Inputting the weekend records would be more exciting. It was a dud.

"This is the way the date went. He was late, as you know. Kitty didn't like him from the git-go. He was so dressed up I felt like a bag lady next to him. I thought we were going to a movie and out to get a bite to eat afterward. I wasn't dressed for a fancy night out. He switched up without telling me. That tells me he's arrogant and into himself. Another thing: he spent the entire night talking about himself. I can't remember one thing he said. Guess I won't be seeing him again." Josie plucked a yellow leaf from a cluster of luscious scarlet geraniums. Rosie listened attentively as she watched her mistress.

"You know what, Rosie? I really love this little house. I didn't think I'd be able to live here again after Mom and Dad died and Kitty twisted my arm to come back here. I miss Baton Rouge so much sometimes I want to cry. There are just too many memories here." The little dog hopped off the porch chair to paw at Josie's leg, a sign she wanted to be picked up and cuddled. Josie obliged.

"C'mon, let's get some coffee. We'll take it out to the porch so we can admire all the pretty flowers. Kitty and I used to play here when we were little. This was originally a potting shed Mom used for her flowers when she did all her gardening. Of course that was before Dad's heart attack and before they went into the catering business. Can you imagine a young man of thirty having a heart attack? It scared Mom silly. When Kitty and I came along she talked Dad into adding a room, and it became our playhouse. We spent whole days out here. We even slept out here sometimes. After we ate our peanut butter and jelly sandwiches we'd spook ourselves and run into the house. Why am I telling you all this? I think it's because Kitty is sick, and I hate it when people get sick. Sometimes when people get sick they . . . they die. It's just a cold. People get colds all the time. In a few days Kitty will be her normal self and cooking up a storm. Things will go back to normal. I worry about everything. I think it has something to do with moving from Baton Rouge three years ago. I miss Mom and Dad. Maybe it has something to do with Kitty getting married the first of next year. I'm just rambling, Rosie. Don't pay attention to anything I say. Here's your baby." Josie fished a Beanie Baby out of her pocket.

The little dog picked up the toy and trotted over to her bed on the corner of the porch. She settled the Beanie Baby between her front paws and proceeded to lick its face. It was a toy she loved and was rarely without. Tears burned

Josie's eyes at the little dog's devotion to her cuddly toy. She should think about getting Rosie a playmate. Something that was alive and breathing. Another dog, or possibly a kitten. It was something to think about.

Not that she didn't have enough to think about. She had plenty of things on her plate, perhaps too many things. Mardi Gras was looming, and she was booked solid for two straight weeks. Then Easter and the usual round of spring parties that led the way to Mother's Day, the busiest time of year. This year they were going to have to hire extra help. She winced when she thought what the extra help would cost her in the way of payroll taxes. They already had four employees, two full-time and two part-time. They were going to need at least four more people to carry them through the summer months. All thanks to *Gourmet Party's* center-spread article.

One article in one glossy magazine, plus their newly designed Web page, and their business had taken off like a rocket. She'd been beating the bushes for a solid year to bring in business—business that had been lost with her parents' death—and now she was so busy she had to turn business away. Dupré Catering's reservation book was full.

Josie saw the car turn into the driveway before Rosie growled. She heard the car door close and then she saw him: a giant of a man, in a business suit. She blinked at his easy stride, noting his dark hair pulled back slickly into a short ponytail. He stopped in midstride, looked down at the ladybug stepping-stones, then looked around, the tiny cottage directly in his line of vision. He closed his eyes and shook his head as though he were shaking off a mirage.

When he realized he was still standing on the ladybug walkway and the cottage was still there, he stepped carefully on the next stone until he was at the foot of the steps leading to the porch.

Good-looking. "Can I help you?" Josie asked as Rosie yipped her way to the top of the steps and growled.

The giant looked down. "Is that a real dog?"

Great body. "Yes. Her name is Rosie. Can I help you?"

The giant placed his right foot on the bottom step. Rosie backed up and lunged. Josie flew off the chair just as a whirlwind of motion streaked up the ladybug walkway and onto the porch. She whirled and was knocked sideways as the tornado crashed into the window boxes, sending them flying through the air. Geraniums and petunias, their clumps of dirt dotted with vermiculite, scattered in all directions, littering the green porch carpet with thousands of specks of white. Rosie's little bed sailed between the rails of the porch, the Beanie Baby flying through the air to land in front of the huge boxer bent on destroying the cottage. Josie watched in horror as the dog's big behind slammed through the screen door. She saw her favorite coffee mug—the one with the cluster of butterflies painted on the side—crash on the front steps. The hanging ferns swung crazily as huge paws swiped at them, finally sending them out into the yard. And then, the ultimate horror, as the huge dog ripped at Rosie's beloved Beanie Baby, causing Josie to give voice to a primal shriek. "Call off your dog, or I will let her rip out your throat!" Later she might laugh at Rosie's vicious hold on the man's pristine white shirt collar. "Look what you did! Stop it this minute! Bite him, Rosie! He ruined her baby! Do you see what he did! She loves that toy. She carries it around all day and sleeps with it. It's worn in. It can't he replaced. Call off your damn dog this minute! I have a gun! I'll get my gun! Give me my dog! Do you hear me? Give me my dog!"

The giant jerked his head backward. He managed to gurgle, "She's yours—just get her the hell off me. She wants my jugular!"

"You want me to try and get past that terrorist! Not in this lifetime, mister. I'm not going to tell you a second time. Give me my dog!"

"She won't let go!"

Overhead a wind chime in one of the trees tinkled to life as a flock of birds took wing. Josie's arms flapped in the air as though she, too, wanted to fly away. "Call off your damn dog! That's an order, mister. Tell him to sit! Tell him *something!*"

"Sit, Zip!"

"Zip?"

"He doesn't listen too well. He's still a puppy," the giant managed to croak.

"A puppy! A puppy! You call that monster a puppy! He's as big as a cow!

"You will now sit, Zip!" Josie thundered. Rosie took that moment to relax her hold on the giant's shirt collar. Two monstrous hands reached up and grasped the little dog around the middle of her body. He held her out in front of him as she snapped and snarled. Zip raised his head and with one swipe of his paw he had the little dog free and between his teeth. He lowered her gently to the littered floor. She ran immediately to her Beanie Baby. Josie watched her as she tried to fix it with her paws, knowing something was seriously wrong. Tears stung Josie's eyes as she dropped to the floor, oblivious to the giant and his dog Zip.

"Shhh, it's okay, Rosie. We'll find the beans. I'll fix it for you. I can sew it up."

"Look, I'm . . ."

"Sorry? Is that what you were going to say? Just get out of here. See, Rosie. I found a few. I'll keep looking. I can sew his head back on. Ohhh, it's going to be okay."

"Can I . . ."

"Help? Your kind of help I don't need."

"I'll pay for the damages. Just tell me how much. I'm sorry. How much do those things cost? Tell me where to get one."

Josie swiveled around. He really was a giant. "Are you dumb or dumb *and* stupid? This can't be replaced. She's had it since she came to me at six weeks. She loves it. It was something to cuddle and cling to when she left her mother. You can't replace something like that. Being a man, you obviously can't be expected to understand."

The trees rustled overhead as the wind chimes tinkled again. A small red bird settled on the railing at the far end of the porch and watched what was going on with bright eyes. Inside the telephone rang as the miniature grandfather clock chimed the hour.

"I thought I told you to leave. Don't bother sending

me a check. Just take your dog and go. Look, Rosie. I found some more beans," Josie crooned soothingly.

"You're still here. What part of 'leave and take your dog with you' didn't you understand?"

"Because I'm a man you think I don't understand the mother-child . . . *thing.*"

"I didn't say anything about a mother and child. I was talking about my dog being taken away from her mother. I'm a person. She's a dog."

The boxer, his eyes dark with misery, loped over to where Rosie was trying to tug her bed from the spokes in the railing. With one bite and one tug, the little bed came free. Rosie hopped in and lay down. The boxer lowered his big head and licked at her tiny face. One giant paw pulled the bed closer to Josie.

"I guess that's an apology from your dog," Josie sputtered. "You need to take him for some obedience courses. You should think about taking a few lessons yourself while you're at it."

"You're pretty mouthy, young lady. My dog was coming to my defense when your dog sprang at me. I told you, he's a puppy. He's not a year old yet. If I had known you had a dog, I would have closed the windows of the car. He didn't get out until your dog did her trapeze act. Does the Board of Health know you have a dog on the premises where food is prepared? You need a sign saying Beware of Dog or something like that. I wasn't expecting a dog."

Out of the corner of her eye, Josie saw the big boxer playing with Rosie. It irritated her. She said so. "Rosie doesn't go in the test kitchens. This is the office, not that it's any of your business. I don't need a dog sign. She's never done anything like that before. She must know you're . . . dangerous or . . . or something."

"I guess I'll be going . . ."

"It's about time," Josie snapped. "Take your dog with you. He looks like he's settling in."

"Are you always this nasty?" the giant asked.

"Yes," Josie snapped again.

"Then I don't think you're the kind of person I want to do business with."

Josie sat back on her haunches, her eyes on the two dogs. Rosie seemed to be enjoying the boxer's attention. They were rubbing noses. Dog love. Was there such a thing?

"Look, you came to me. I didn't come to you. You are certainly within your rights to do business wherever you like. I would like to remind you that it was your dog who did all this. I'm willing to chalk it up as one of those unexpected things that happen every so often. I can replace the plants and rehang the window boxes. The screen door will have to be redone. It's cleanup, basically. With the exception of Rosie's toy. Why don't we just forget this happened and go on from there?"

"Fine. Come on, Zip, time to go home."

Josie watched the big dog out of the corner of her eye. He wasn't moving, and it didn't look like he was about to move either. Obviously the giant was of the same opinion. She did her best to hide her smile when he leaned over and picked up the huge dog, who protested mightily by howling his head off. Rosie whined and yipped as she ran after the giant and his dog. Josie ran after them, only to meet up with Kitty in the driveway.

"My God!" the giant exclaimed. "There are two of you!"

"What's he talking about, Josie? What's going on? Somebody tell me something."

"Later," Josie said, scooping up the little dog, who only wanted to get in the backseat of the car with the big dog.

Thanks to Zip's huge paws, the horn of the Mercedes sedan blasted again and again as the giant backed the car out of the driveway. The picture of the giant and his big dog driving the fancy Mercedes would stay with Josie for a long time. She grinned as Rosie whined all the way back to the cottage.

"Don't panic now, Kitty. I'll clean it all up. It's a good thing it's Monday. What are you doing out of bed?"

"Who was that? He looks familiar. Oh, my God! What happened?"

"His dog got loose, and Rosie went for his throat—the guy, not the dog. I don't know what he wanted, and I don't even know what his name was . . . is. Go back to bed, and I'll clean this up. The dog got Rosie's Beanie Baby. I have to find the beans. Maybe I can sew it up. I don't even want to think about tonight if she doesn't have it to sleep with. By the way, what *are* you doing out of bed?"

"When you didn't pick up the phone in the cottage, I

answered it in the house. It was Mrs. Lobelia. She wants to know if she can come over to talk to you this afternoon. Something about that big party she's planning for Mother's Day. I told her yes since we have nothing scheduled for today. Older people like to do things right away. They don't like to wait around. Okay, okay, I'm going back inside."

Josie stared at her twin. It was the same as staring at herself in the mirror. They had the same dark brown eyes, the same dimples, the same jawline, and identical noses. Their hair was brown and curly, with no options for style, and it left little for people to tell them apart. Even the giant had recognized that they were identical.

Kitty had been her best friend from the moment their mother had placed them together in the same crib. It was them against the world, or so it had seemed at the time. Two voices were always better as well as louder. At least they got to be heard. They had played all the standard twin tricks, and for a time in their teens they were able to fool their parents a time or two.

Kitty was the serious, stable one. Kitty was the one who thought things through and always came up with the right answer, and it was Kitty who loved to cook. Unlike Josie, who couldn't boil water. Josie was what Kitty called a loose cannon, flying off the handle, plowing ahead and reading directions after she broke whatever it was she was trying to put together. She had a head for business, unlike Kitty, who said it bored her to tears. They were a natural, as Kitty put it, to take over their parents' catering firm. She would do the cooking, and Josie would handle the business end of it. Now, three years later, their books were solidly in the black. "The American dream," Kitty had said back in Baton Rouge when she wanted Josie to agree to take over the business. "We answer to no one but ourselves. We give ourselves the best health insurance, the best pension plan, and we don't have to worry about anyone downsizing or snatching it away from us." Josie had agreed because it made sense. She liked being her own boss. She'd hated the bank she worked in just the way Kitty hated the insurance company she worked for.

She loved N'awlins, or the Big Easy, as people called the city. She adored the Garden District, with its wonderful old homes like their own, as well as the exciting French Quarter. When she missed Baton Rouge, the city where she and Kitty first achieved their independence, she hopped in the car and drove there, sometimes at a moment's notice. As Kitty said, the past was prologue. N'awlins was her home again just the way it had been her home growing up.

"Get to bed," she ordered her sister. "I'll meet with Mrs. Lobelia, but first I have to clean up the porch and see about fixing Rosie's baby."

"Why don't you go to the store, buy another Beanie Baby, take out the beans, and sew it up again? I'll take Rosie in the house with me so she won't see you doing it."

"That's a thought, but only if I can't find the beans. I want to fix it for her just the way it was. I'll be in to fix lunch in a little while."

"The guy was a hunk. A real pity you didn't get his

name. Bet he works out or runs. His muscles positively rippled when he was carrying that big dog." Kitty grinned.

"You saw all that through his suit?"

"Yep. Those eyes are to drown in. Very kissable mouth. His teeth positively *glistened.*"

"I didn't notice," Josie muttered.

"Get off it, Josie. You noticed. No good-looking man gets by that eagle eye of yours. By the way, how'd the date go last night?"

"First and last. He was just too full of himself. Get that matchmaking look out of your eye. I'd never date a man who has hair longer than my own. Cajun, Choctaw maybe. What do you think?"

"Maybe a combination. Whatever it is, it works. He was one handsome guy. I've seen him somewhere. It will come to me sooner or later. That was no off-the-rack suit he was wearing either, and that car isn't exactly a puddle-jumper. Big bucks. Pity you let him get away," Kitty said as she flounced her way up the steps.

Was it a pity? Josie wondered as she made her way to the cottage, where she worked industriously gathering up as many of the tiny beans as she could find. Two hours later she had the soft little toy sewn together. She bent over Rosie, who was curled into a ball in her little bed. "Here you go, baby, good as new." She wanted to cry when the Maltese made no effort to reach for it to cuddle with as she always did. "I think I got all the beans. See, it's just as fat and wiggly as before. C'mere." The little dog made no effort to move but buried her head in her paws.

Damn, if she could get her hands around the giant's throat, she would squeeze the life out of him. And his monster dog. Her best hope was that Kitty would remember where she'd seen him so she could then go and wring his big neck. Like that was really going to happen.

The ferns looked a little sparse when she rehung them, but with more potting soil and a good spritzing they looked almost as good as new. She did her best with the geraniums and petunias, but most of the stems were broken and bent. She needed new ones. How bare and impersonal the little porch looked without the colorful blooms. She was going to have to remove the screen door and take it to be repaired. She might as well do that now and pick up some new flowers on the way back. She had plenty of time before her meeting with Mrs. Lobelia. She could also pick up a couple of po'boys for lunch for her and Kitty.

"Come on, Rosie. Help me take off this screen door and then we'll go in the car. Hop to it, girl." When the little dog didn't move, Josie bent down to pick her up. The dog didn't protest, but she didn't do her usual wiggle and squirm routine, either.

It was after the noon hour when Josie parked the van outside Franky and Johnny's on Arabella Street. She cracked the window and locked the doors while she went inside to order Kitty's favorite po'boy. She ordered two of the hefty sandwiches made with local French bread filled with roast beef, fried shrimp, oysters, ham, or meatballs, with cheese, and gravy or tomato sauce. She told them to "dress" it, which meant they would add lettuce, mayonnaise, and mustard with a slice of tomato. She knew they would butter the bread and heat it just the way she and her sister liked it.

She heard Rosie yapping and clawing at the window the minute she closed the door of the restaurant. She ran to the car and unlocked it. Normally the little dog would try to pry open the bag and sniff out the contents. Right now all she wanted was to get out of the Ford Explorer.

She saw it then as her gaze swept the street. Down the block, the sleek, expensive Mercedes was parked at the curb. In the blink of an eye, Rosie leaped over Josie's lap and jumped to the ground. She sprinted down the street, Josie in pursuit.

Josie watched in amazement as the little dog tried to scale the car door. On one of her jumps, Josie reached out and grabbed her in midair. In doing so she could see the interior of the car clearly. It was ripped to shreds, the fine leather hanging in strips, the rearview mirror half off its track. There was no sign of the owner or his dog. Obviously, Rosie was picking up the boxer's scent.

He came out of nowhere, the big dog dragging him forward. With one mighty lunge, the boxer tore loose of the giant's grip on his leash. He bounded over to the curb to where Josie was standing with Rosie, skidded to a stop, sat up on his hind legs, and whined for Josie to set the little dog down. Before Josie could make up her mind, Rosie wiggled free and leaped to the ground, where the boxer nuzzled and playfully prodded her with one of his big paws.

The giant cleared his throat. "It would seem we have a bit of a problem."

Kitty was right. He is definitely a hunk. "I'd certainly second that," Josie said, pointing to the inside of the elegant car. "When did he do that?"

"He did the backseat on the way from your place and the front when I tried to take him to that dog school down the block. He almost chewed off the steering wheel," the giant said in disgust. "He wants something. I don't know what the something is. Did you get your dog's toy fixed?"

"Yes, but she doesn't want it. She wouldn't even touch it. Ah . . . the reason I'm standing here is she must have picked up . . . his scent. That's the only thing I can figure out. I was in Franky and Johnny's to pick up some po'boys, and she was going wild. I came to see what it was she wanted. I guess it's your dog. I have to go now. Can you put your dog in your car so we can leave?"

"I'll try. He's not going to like it," the giant said. "Maybe you should leave first."

"He'll follow us. You go first. If the doors are closed, he can't get out. Can he?" Josie asked tartly.

"He'll probably go through the damn window. Is that fur ball in heat?" the giant asked suspiciously.

"No, the fur ball is not in heat. She's spayed. I resent you calling her a fur ball. She has a name, and it's Rosalie—Rosie for short. What about yours?"

"He's fixed, too. Maybe they like the way the other smells. Yours smells like coconut. I can't believe my dog likes that prissy smell."

"Well your dog smells like a wet wool sweater a cat peed on. I can't believe my dog would be attracted to such a smell."

"Enough!" the giant roared. "Get in the car, Zip. Don't make me pick you up again." Zip continued to nuzzle Rosie. Josie watched in amusement.

"Pick yours up at the same time," the giant ordered in an authoritative voice.

Josie bristled, but did as instructed.

"Now run like hell!" the giant roared.

Josie ran, the little dog barking and squirming to get out of her grasp. She wanted to look behind her but was afraid she would lose her momentum and somehow Rosie would get loose from her grasp. She was breathing like a long-distance runner when she finally plopped down in the driver's seat, the van securely locked. She turned to look at the huddled dog on the passenger seat next to her. "Listen, little girl. I don't know what the hell that was all about, but we aren't going to go through it again. That dog is just too big for you to play with. He's the one who tore your precious baby. I'm the one who fixed it, and now you don't even want it. Snap out of it. Zip went home. We're going home. This is the end of it."

Josie put the Explorer in gear and turned around in the middle of the road. She sensed rather than saw the Mercedes doing the same thing. *Good, we're going in opposite directions.* She was almost to Jackson Square when she realized she still didn't know the giant's name. What difference did it make if she knew his name or not? Life would go on regardless. The sun would come up tomorrow and the day after tomorrow. He was a hunk, though. She laughed aloud when she remembered the interior of the luxury vehicle. Big dogs, big damage.

Josie turned left on Prytania Street continuing down until she crossed Washington Street and then Fourth Street. She turned right on Third Street and drove into her driveway. She was home.

As always, she was struck with the beauty of the old pillared house shrouded with live oaks. They'd had the house painted last October, and it gleamed now in the bright noonday sun. She heard rather than saw a tour bus with the guide shouting out tidbits about the Garden District and the people who lived inside the beautiful old buildings. He would take them past the home of Anne Rice of vampire fame. Everyone would ooh and aaah over the huge stone wolf on her second-floor balcony. Then the guide would tell them about the church she bought before he took them past Tulane and Loyola's campuses. Just another sight-seeing day in N'awlins.

The front porch was alive with plants and hanging ferns, all in need of watering. Perhaps later, after the sun went down. For now she had to go inside. With Rosie in one hand and the po'boys in the other, she somehow managed to fit the key into the lock of the majestic teakwood door. She slammed it shut immediately and then locked it, secure in the knowledge that Rosie couldn't get out.

While the house was old, her parents had kept up with it, and so had she and Kitty. Just last year they'd painted inside and out, and it still looked fresh and clean. They'd discarded a lot of their parents' old comfortable furniture and replaced it with more modern but just as comfortable love seats and easy chairs. The long windows still had their swagged draperies. They'd kept the old rugs because to do away with them would have been sacrilegious. The shiny, worn pine floors and the breathtaking staircase made of solid teak were wonders that caused visitors to gasp in delight. Or perhaps it was the high ceilings or the ornate woodwork.

"Anybody home? I brought lunch. You'll never guess what I bought. And you'll never guess who I ran into," Josie called from the foot of the stairway. "What do you want to drink? Cola, sweet tea, or a cold beer?"

"Sweet tea," Kitty called from the top of the staircase. "You went uptown and got po'boys from Franky and Johnny's. I bet you ran into the hunk. Howzat for guessing with a stuffed-up head? Did he ask you out?"

"No, he did not ask me out. It wasn't that kind of meeting. Rosie knew they were there. You should see what his dog did to that expensive car he drives, and no, I still don't know his name."

"I know him from somewhere," Kitty grumbled. "When are you going to get the screen door back? I love that screen door. I like the way it bangs shut, and I like the way it squeaks no matter what you do to it. Mom said it was supposed to do that because it was an old-fashioned wooden screen door, not like those aluminum things. I can't believe that dog put his big rear end through our screen door."

"You up to these po'boys, Kitty. How's your throat?"

"Never mind my throat. Tell me about the hunk."

Josie told her. "See for yourself. Rosie wants nothing to do with me. She wouldn't even touch the Beanie Baby.

All she wants is that damn big dog and, what's worse, he wants her. How is that possible, Kitty, since they've both been fixed?"

"Ummnn. Beats me. Before I forget, a package came while you were out. It's in the hall under the table."

Josie unwrapped the po'boys and set them on what her mother called her day dishes—plain, heavy white china with a large, succulent strawberry in the middle. There were only four left in the entire set, aside from two cups and two soup bowls. The matching napkins were old and faded, but neither girl was willing to part with them.

It was a cheerful kitchen, with wraparound windows and a cozy breakfast nook. Perfect for morning coffee, newspaper reading, and bird-watching. The Hansel and Gretel cottage and the ladybug walkway were clearly visible from each window, something that brought a smile to each young woman's face no matter what time of day.

Kitty poured the sweet tea from her great-grandmother's crystal pitcher.

"Who's the package from?" Josie asked as she bit into her po'boy.

"*Gourmet Party*. Probably more copies of their magazine. Maybe it's a hint that we should subscribe. We should, you know. The publicity that centerfold gave us is invaluable. Maybe they want us to hand them out to our customers. It felt kind of light, though."

"Okay, I'll take out a subscription. Any phone calls?"

"Not a one. Seems like everyone goes underground on Monday. Too much partying on Bourbon Street over the weekend. So, get the box and open it already. Let's see what they sent us. If it is magazines, you can give one to Mrs. Lobelia when she comes over."

Josie walked into the hallway, looking over her shoulder to see if Rosie would follow her. Her heart thumped in her chest when the little dog stayed under the kitchen table. She picked up the box. Kitty was right: It was light. She was curious now. Her sandwich could wait.

Kitty watched as Josie slit the top of the packing box with a sharp knife. She dug down into the bubble wrap and pulled out a stuffed animal. "It's a boxer! What in the world?"

"Now I know where I saw the hunk!" Kitty cried. "He's in the same magazine we were in but he's in the back end of it. When we first got it, I was like you. I just read our own article and chortled a bit. Then one day, I was leafing through it, and there he was. It isn't nearly as grand as the one they did on us. That dog you're holding is his. The same one who ran amuck on the cottage. What does the note say? Hurry up, read it."

The Maltese came out from under the table and yipped her pleasure at the sight of the huge stuffed animal. "Would you look at that," Josie whispered to her sister. The little dog used her snout to topple the animal until it fell over. She bit down on one of the pointed ears and dragged it to her bed at the far side of the kitchen. She tilted her head to the side to see what her mistress thought of the situation. Josie clapped her hands and said, "Good girl, Rosie."

"I was starting to worry about her. Do you think they sent the boxer to us by mistake and ours went to . . . *him*?"

"I'd say that's a logical assumption. What does the card say?"

"Just that they enjoyed working with us and they wanted to send this small gift as a token of their appreciation. One of their employees makes stuffed animals. That's all it says."

"Wow! What do you think he'll say when he gets ours? Do you think he'll bring it back? You could call the magazine and get his address. They'll give it to you when you tell them about the mistake."

"I will do no such thing. I'm not taking that away from Rosie. Look at her—she loves it. Where's the magazine? I want to see what it says about him."

"I thought you weren't interested."

"I'm not. I just want to read it."

"You're going to have to wait. I hear a car, so that must mean Mrs. Lobelia is here. Mrs. Lobelia with lots of money."

"Save that article for me, Kitty. I'll read it later. You know what? Just for the heck of it, go ahead and call the magazine and get his address."

"Just for the heck of it, huh?"

"Yeah, just for the heck of it. You never know. That screen door might turn out to be an expensive proposition. I had to order new hardware. And I had to get new screws for the window boxes. New plants. That adds up. I might want to change my mind and send him a bill."

"Sounds like a plan to me. Consider it done."

Two

Josie took one last bite from her po'boy before she ran to the hallway mirror to check her appearance. She tweaked the curls falling over her forehead, pinched her cheeks for a little extra color, and smoothed down the long linen skirt. New clients deserved a good presentation. Then she remembered the condition of the cottage floor, with all the dirt and the fluffy vermiculite that dotted the green outdoor carpeting. "It is what it is," she muttered as she skipped her way down the ladybug walkway.

She was tiny, so tiny at first glance that Josie thought she was a child. She wasn't just pretty—she was gorgeous, with her high coronet of snow-white braids and flawless complexion. *Seventy if she's a day, a youthful seventy,* Josie thought. There was a springiness to her step, and she was dressed in a swirling, colorful skirt with matching top. A straw hat with oversize sunglasses dangled from one hand, a Chanel bag from the other. She wore the diamonds in her ears and on her fingers like royalty. Josie estimated the total carat weight at around twelve or so. Possibly more. Brilliant straw sandals with two-inch heels and a diamond ankle bracelet completed her attire.

Marie Lobelia smiled warmly, her eyes twinkling. Josie fell in love with her at that moment. She fought the urge to take her in her arms for a bone-crushing hug.

"I love this," the little woman said, waving her arms about. "It's so peaceful, so colorful. I had no idea this was even back here." She waved her arms again to indicate the cottage and the long, square building that made up the kitchens and catering center.

"My sister and I have only been here three years. Our parents operated the catering service until their death. There was a gas-line explosion that killed them. This has all been redone and landscaped. We added more flowers, some shrubbery, and we repainted the ladybugs and the cottage. I apologize for the condition of the carpet, but we had a bit of an accident this morning. I had to take the screen door to the hardware store for repairs and didn't get to the floor. Step carefully."

The little woman waved her arms again to show that the condition of the floor was of no importance. She stepped through the door. "Was this building always here?" she twinkled.

"Yes. It was originally a potting shed, and when my sister and I were born, my mother had a room added to it and it became our playhouse. There are some wonderful memories attached to this little house. However, my parents never used it the way Kitty and I do. They had offices in the building in the back."

"It's cozy and comfortable," Marie Lobelia said, sitting down in a white wicker rocking chair. "I've heard good things about your catering service," she said, getting right to the point. "I called several times last year, but you were always booked up. I'd like to engage your services for two events. I want to host a small party on the Epiphany and of course I want the traditional King Cake. Tradition these days is to bake a tiny baby doll representing the baby Jesus into the cake, and whoever gets that particular piece hosts the next King Cake party. I prefer the old way. A pecan will do nicely in place of the baby doll. I want the traditional colors of Mardi Gras, green, yellow, and purple sugars used. I'm sure you've done this hundreds of times. I just like to make sure things are clear from the beginning."

"I grew up here, Mrs. Lobelia. My mother always made a King Cake for us on the Epiphany. There were parties every night until Mardi Gras ended. Now, tell me what else you would like for your party. How many guests?" Josie asked, her pencil posed.

"A dozen or so. The usual: jambalaya, gumbo, etouffée, praline pie. Go easy on the Andouille since our stomachs aren't what they used to be. I hope you have a good roux recipe. I prefer a dark roux. I want it all to be authentic. I'll leave the appetizers up to you."

Josie scribbled furiously. "I have some excellent recipes. Before I make a decision, I'll consult with you. You mentioned another engagement."

The diamonds on the tiny hands winked under the soft lighting. Josie leaned back in her swivel chair to better observe the little woman's agitation at the simple statement.

"Yes. I'm not sure . . . What I mean is . . . I might possibly be making a mistake . . . It seems like the right thing to do and yet . . . Yes, I want to engage your services for a Mother's Day party. A gala of sorts if seventy- and eighty-year-old people can experience such a thing without falling asleep. You see, I want to do this for . . . for my family. By that I mean relatives who no longer have children or whose children have . . . forgotten about them. Several cousins won't make it past the new year, so I thought . . . It's such a special day. Perhaps I'm wrong to do this. What is your opinion, chère?"

"I think it's a wonderful thing to be remembered on Mother's Day. My sister and I always tried to do something special for Mom. We'd pick flowers, serve her toast in bed. We weren't allowed to make anything else when we were younger. We'd sing her a song we learned in school. She'd clap her hands and hug us. They were the best hugs," Josie said, with a catch in her voice. "Do you have children of your own, Mrs. Lobelia?"

"I did," Marie said flatly. "My oldest daughter died in childbirth. Her husband moved away and took the child with him. She'd be about your age now. I've never seen or heard from them since that day. My second daughter died at the age of sixteen from cystic fibrosis. My son . . . my son operates our family business out of our corporate headquarters in New York. I never see him. He calls on occasion. I can't change things. I'm not sure I would even if I could. Everything in life is preordained. Do you believe that, chère?"

How sad she is. What could be worse than having no

family? "Yes, I do agree. Now, tell me what it is you would like for your Mother's Day party."

"Since it's going to be the same group of ladies, I think we'll need a different menu. I'll take care of the gifts and the flowers. Every mother should get flowers on Mother's Day. How hard is it to send a card?"

Josie pretended not to see the tears gathering in the faded caramel-colored eyes. She looked down at the paper in front of her. "I think my sister and I can make this a very special day for you and your friends. Let me talk to Kitty, and I'll run the details by you before we make any definite decisions. Is there anything else I can do for you?"

"I don't know if you know this or not, but I still own and operate a small company that my first husband and I started. We package cornmeal and print a new recipe each quarter on our bags. I've run out of recipes. I'd like something new and unique. I'm afraid the company is faltering a bit. I need something to perk it up. I don't want my son to come back and snatch it away from me because he thinks I'm seventy-four years old and not capable of operating the company. Right now we're holding our own. I've found over the years that a new recipe drives up sales. Do you think you could come up with something? Name your price."

What kind of son did this sweet woman have? A shark. "This is just off the top of my head, Mrs. Lobelia, but have you given any thought to, say, a bake-off or cook-off, something like that. More important, do you have a Web page? If not, I know someone who can design one for you. Perhaps a dish that could be written up and prepared at someplace like the Commander's Palace or possibly Emeril Lagasse's restaurant if you go with the cook-off idea?"

"Now you're cookin', chère. What a fabulous idea! I don't want to be a failure at my age. Now, why didn't I think of that? I'll need the recipe by April first. I can't wait to tell the girls. The Web page sounds wonderful. I'll do it. Will that be a problem?"

Josie smiled. "I don't think so. Are you Cajun, Mrs. Lobelia? Lobelia isn't a Cajun-sounding name."

"Lobelia is Choctaw. However, I am Cajun. I've been married four times. Somehow I managed to outlive all four husbands. I come from sturdy stock as they say. Oh my goodness, we didn't discuss payment. Let me just write you a check as a deposit and then you can send me a bill for the rest. Will that be satisfactory?"

"This is our price list. You might want to look at it when you have time. Twenty percent is customary. We can work out the payment for the recipe later on. It's been nice doing business with you," Josie said, accepting the scribbled check. Her eyes widened. "This is too much, Mrs. Lobelia."

"It's fine. Don't worry about it. Just post it to my account. Do you mind if I ask you a question?"

"Not at all."

"Was your mother perfect? Was she a perfect mother? You know, one of those June Cleaver types."

Josie laughed. "I don't think there's any such thing as a perfect mother. But, to answer your question, no, she wasn't perfect. She had flaws. She made mistakes. She knew how to apologize, and she gave the best hugs. That made up for everything because my sister and I knew she loved us."

"I guess that's where it all went wrong," Marie Lobelia murmured. "My son wanted a perfect mother. Call me, chère. My phone number is on the check. I can see my way out. You need a screen door, chère."

Josie laughed again. "It's being repaired. It's one of those old-fashioned wooden ones that squeak."

"The best kind. I used to love hearing it slam when the children were little. Someone was always poking a hole in it. One day it would be new and the next day it would have a strip of adhesive tape over the hole and the little wires would poke through. I'm surprised I remember that. I do ramble. I'm sorry. It's what happens when you get old. Senior moments." She giggled and then took her leave.

"Whoever your son is, Mrs. Lobelia, he's a *shit*!" Josie muttered when she was alone. "Perfect mother my foot!"

Josie leaned back in her swivel chair and closed her eyes. They snapped open so she could stare down at the check in the amount of $20,000. A good day's work by any standard. She should go to the bank. Or she could go up to the house and look at the article in *Gourmet Party* magazine. On the other hand, she could do both. She could go to the bank *and* read the article.

Josie tidied her desk, turned off her computer and the lights, her head filled with memories of when she and Kitty held tea parties and dance classes in these very rooms. How often she'd run here with Kitty when a punishment was something she didn't think she could bear. Once she and Kitty had made curtains for the diamond-shaped windows. Just squares of brightly colored cloth held together with safety pins. They'd been so proud of those curtains. Now, crisp, crisscross organdy curtains hung on the shiny windows. There were no teddy bears and dolls with stretched-out, matted hair on the window seats. The soft, cuddly pillows perfect for holding against one's chest were gone, too, replaced with custom-made flowered cushions.

A red wagon, its wheels rusted, had sat next to a blue tricycle in the corner of the room. Stacks of building blocks, every color of the rainbow, nestled in discarded orange-mesh bags. She wondered what happened to the tin tea set with the violets painted in the center. Maybe her mother threw it out when the pieces started to rust around the edges.

Memories. Mrs. Lobelia must have memories like hers. Sad memories. Sad memories she had to live with.

Josie closed and locked the Dutch door, which matched the diamond-shaped panes in the front windows. She missed the screen door. She really had to sweep the porch. Just the thought of cleaning all the tiny white specks made her shudder. Maybe the leaf blower would be the answer. It would be something to do later after she went to the bank and after she read the article in the magazine.

"What's for dinner, Josie?" Kitty asked.

"The rest of the po'boys and some canned soup. We're twenty thousand dollars richer today, sister dear. That makes me feel good. Real good. It surprised me that Mrs. Lobelia knew about the column I write for the *Gazette* during Lent. You know, the one where you come up with a recipe every week and I pass it off as mine. The column gave her the idea for the recipe on her cornmeal bag. I'm impressed." Then she told her sister her ideas for Mrs. Lobelia's company.

"The Commander's Palace and Emeril Lagasse! For a cook-off! How do you expect to pull that off?" Kitty queried as she sipped at her hot rum tea.

"I just threw that out as a suggestion. It sounded good at the time, and she was expecting me to say something. It isn't carved in stone. We've always been good at improvising. If it's not that, then it will be something else. Hey, maybe a picnic at Evangeline Oak, the legendary meeting place of Emmeline and Louis. You remember Longfellow's poem *Evangeline*, don't you? It's the true story of Emmeline Labiche and Louis Arceneaux, two lovers who were separated for years before finally reuniting. Everyone loves that story and going to that old oak. Like I said, it's a thought. By the way, how are you feeling?"

"A little tired, but I think that's from blowing my nose every ten minutes. I'm over the worst of it. I'll be back in the kitchen tomorrow. You read the article, and I'll heat the soup and warm the sandwiches. Hey, look at Rosie," Kitty hissed.

Josie looked under the table. Rosie was sound asleep, her little head cradled between the stuffed animal's paws. Josie smiled.

"Nice article. Not as good as ours. Guess that's why he got the back and we got the centerfold. The camera likes him. Good bone structure. He doesn't look like he knows how to relax. Kind of stiff-looking. The arrogance is there, though. If he's Cajun, what happened to his accent? It says here he's Cajun. He must have a lot of money. He has a house right here in the Garden District, a chalet in Switzerland, and a house in the Hamptons. That all makes for big bucks. They stop short of saying he's a playboy. Old money. It doesn't say what it is exactly that he does. We do have a name now, though. Paul Brouillette. We could look him up in the phone book. If we were interested, that is. Since we aren't interested, we won't look it up," Josie said.

"I already did that. I wrote the number on the pad by the phone. Just in case we wanted to call him, which we don't, so we probably should throw away the number," Kitty said breathlessly.

"You already called the number, didn't you?" Josie said suspiciously.

Kitty winked at her sister. "I just wanted to see if he was home. He wasn't. His answering machine came on. I hung up. There's nothing wrong with that. I wanted to be sure he was bona fide in case we have to, you know, send him a bill for the screen door like you said. It wouldn't hurt you to show a little interest. I'll bet you could get him just by snapping your fingers. If you're interested, that is," Kitty said slyly as she ladled soup into the two strawberry bowls.

"I can't believe you're trying to match me up with some . . . Cajun playboy with a ponytail. Let's get real here, and you know what else? I am going to send him a bill for the repairs regardless of the cost. The plants were over a hundred dollars. The screen door is going to be at least sixty. I had to buy screws for the windows boxes. It damn well adds up."

"Why don't you take the bill over there personally? Gee whiz, you could walk from here. Give Rosie a chance to wreck his place."

"I'm not giving back that stuffed dog. That's a given. Look how happy she is. We don't ever mention that, okay, Kitty?"

"Fine by me. You make it sound like we're going to be seeing him again. How's that going to happen?" Her voice turned sly again as she raised her eyes to the slowly rotating paddle fan over the kitchen table. "I think it's gonna rain."

"Don't change the subject. The weatherman didn't say anything about rain. That gray cloud over the backyard is going to go away."

"When we were little we used to pray for rain so we could slop in the puddles and make mud pies," Kitty said wistfully. "I don't care if I am all grown-up. I want to do that again. I wonder what it would be like to run naked through the rain sucking on a mango."

Josie choked on the food in her mouth. "Where . . . what . . . ?"

"I asked Harry if he ever did that and he said no but he had crawled buck-ass naked through tall weeds sucking on a long neck bottle of Budweiser. I thought it was kind of funny. We're going to do it the next time it rains. Providing I'm recovered from my cold."

"Thanks for sharing that with me," Josie said hoarsely. Kitty would do it, too. Kitty was the adventuresome one. The most daring thing Josie had ever done with a guy was to go skinny-dipping. Because she was two minutes older, she felt as though she had to set an example for her more precocious twin. Some example.

"I'll clean up. Start thinking about a new recipe for Mrs. Lobelia. I'm going to take Rosie for a walk."

"I drew a kind of crude map of where Mr. Rich lives. It's on the sheet under his phone number. Just go to the end of this street, make a right and two lefts, and *voilà,* you're there."

Josie threw the dishtowel at her sister's back. She tucked the directions in the back of her mind. Not that she had any intention of following them. Besides, how could she possibly know the house number? She looked around to see if Kitty was within eye range. Satisfied, she peeked under the first sheet of paper on the notepad. There it was: 2899. How hard could that be to remember? She tucked it away in her mind along with the directions.

Ninety minutes later, Josie tripped down the staircase, Rosie's leash in her hand.

Kitty whistled her appreciation from her position on the couch. "Nice dog-walking outfit! Isn't that the same getup you spent days searching for when you had a date with that diplomat not too long ago? Didn't you say you were sick for days over how much it cost? Is that perfume I smell? By God, it is perfume!" Kitty said sniffing appreciatively. "It *is* the same perfume you bought for that tight-assed diplomat who arm wrestled you on the front porch. You're lookin' good, girl. He'd be a fool to turn you down."

"I simply changed my clothes because I dribbled some

of the tomato soup on my blouse. I'm not going anywhere near his house. Stop matchmaking. The diplomat was a jerk. I might as well get some use out of this outfit. As for the perfume, I like it. What's wrong with wearing perfume?"

"Are you going to gussy up Rosie, too?"

"I put a clean bow in her hair. I do that every day. Get that gleam out of your eye, Kitty. You're up to something, aren't you? You wouldn't dare! Tell me you wouldn't . . ."

"Me pretend to be you and go visit him! Nah! That's kid stuff. We're all grown-up now. Besides, I can't get pissed off like you do. I'm too easygoing. He'd see right through the charade."

Josie jiggled the leash and waited for Rosie to join her. When Rosie finally wiggled her way through the dining room to the living room she had the stuffed dog with her.

"Look at her." Kitty laughed. "She's exhausted from dragging that toy. Looks like you're going to have to pull her in the wagon. From the looks of her she won't last a block, and you have about four to go from the front door."

"You're out of your mind! There's no way I'm going to pull a dog in a wagon down the street. People are sitting on their porches. They'll laugh me right out of town."

Josie flopped down on the couch next to her sister. "I miss that old couch with the spring popping through at the end. We should have kept it. Since my plans have been thwarted, I think I'll have a little glass of wine or maybe a tall beer. How about you, Kitty?"

"Beer sounds good. Turn the fans on when you get

back. It's getting hot already. I hate humidity. My hair is nothing but a ball of frizz. I'm going to get some of that stuff that takes the curl out of your hair."

"Don't bother. It doesn't work," Josie said, handing her a beer. "Kitty, was Mom anywhere near being a perfect mother?"

"Not to my way of thinking. Why do you ask?"

Josie told her about Mrs. Lobelia and her son. "I don't even know anyone who has a perfect mother. More to the point, what *is* a perfect mother?"

Kitty shrugged as she gulped at the frosty beer. "I guess it's someone who does everything right, anticipates your every need, is always there, never complains, and always smiles no matter what. Jeez, Mom was nothing like that. Remember how she used to whip our asses with the wooden spoon when we did something wrong? To me, that's a perfect mother. She wanted us to know right from wrong. We never made the same mistake twice, so I guess it worked. How about another beer since you aren't going for your walk?"

"Sure, why not?" Josie said glumly. She hated taking these trips down Memory Lane.

The twins were finishing their second bottle of beer when the phone rang. "Right on schedule," Josie muttered. "The guy is a creature of habit. Does he *ever* call at two minutes past the hour? Does he have some kind of timer he goes by? Where's the excitement? How can you get an adrenaline rush when you know he's going to call precisely at eight o'clock? If you want my opinion, your intended is boring as hell. I'm going for that walk now while you talk about nothing for two hours."

"The wagon's by the front door. Rosie is waiting for you," Kitty gurgled. "Don't worry. No one will see you since it's getting dark."

Rosie yipped her pleasure. Going out the front door in the wagon was something new. Normally, Josie pulled her around in the garden. She yipped again before she cuddled with the stuffed dog. "We're just going up the street and down the street. I have a buzz on and . . . I probably shouldn't even be out. Maybe halfway down the block. Halfway is good. That's what we'll do."

It was a beautiful, quiet evening, the air clear and fresh, the sky full of stars. Even though it was getting dark, Josie could make out quiet forms sitting on front porches. Some of the neighbors waved or shouted an evening greeting. She waved back. The jasmine smelled heavenly that evening. Once she'd bought a bottle of expensive perfume called Jasmine and had been so disappointed with the bottled scent she'd thrown it away.

Josie was about to turn the wagon around at the end of the block when she heard the crunch and grind of rusty wheels. She stepped to the side and reached for the lamppost just as a tall form pulling something behind him rounded the corner. *Him.* It was instant chaos. Whatever he was pulling slammed into the man, pushing him forward until he, too, was hanging on to the lamppost. The boxer leaped and pranced as Rosie yipped and danced her way around him. Traffic crawled by as teenagers whooped and hollered.

"We have to stop meeting like this," the man said huskily, one eye on the girl pinned under his arms and one on the dogs' wild antics.

"Why?" *Brilliant. Absolutely brilliant. Keep your mouth closed so he doesn't smell your breath.*

"Meeting twice in one day like this is . . . rather strange, don't you think?"

"Is that what you say to all the women you meet? Is that dog of yours some kind of shill or something? Ooops," she gurgled as she lost her balance. She righted herself and hung on to the light pole. *Damn, now he was going to think she was a drunk. So much for the pricey outfit and the sinful perfume.*

"Miss Dupré, are you by any chance . . . ah, inebriated?"

"Do I look in . . . inebr . . . drunk?" *Go ahead, keep giving him more clues.* "Where's your Cajun accent, you . . . you Cajun playboy? I read all about you. I did. So did my sister."

"I lost my accent went I went north to school. It didn't go over very well at Princeton. I'm not a playboy, but I do like to play. I'm flattered that you read my article. I read yours, too. Why don't I walk you home? You seem a bit unsteady. Do you have any more questions?" he asked patiently.

Did she? She wished she could think straight. Swinging around the lamppost certainly wasn't doing her any good. "As a matter of fact I do have a question. What's your definition of a perfect mother, sir?"

He took so long to reply, Josie prodded him as she

peered at him in the yellowish light from the lamp. She wasn't so tipsy that she couldn't see the misery in his eyes or the slump of his shoulder. "Well?"

"Probably someone who knows her son's name, makes him breakfast, kisses him good-bye before she sends him off to school and listens to his prayers at night when she tucks him in. Are you writing a book?" he asked stiffly.

"My mother was like that, but she wasn't perfect. It has to be more than that. I might write a book. The idea . . . intri . . . intrigues me." Josie hiccuped.

"Come along, Miss Dupré. I'll walk you home. Do you think you can pull the wagon, or should I do it for you? It's amazing that we were both doing the same thing. Zip likes to ride in the wagon. I guess I'm just a sucker for dogs. May I say you look lovely this evening."

"This is my dog-walking outfit. I bought it for that . . . diplomat. He had diplomatic immunity. They can get away with *anything*. I gave him a black eye and bit him on the neck. I'm going to throw it away."

"That sounds like it might be a good idea."

"Why?"

"Because it brings to mind an unhappy experience. By the way, I got a stuffed dog in the mail today that was obviously meant for you."

"Yeah, well, I got yours, too, and I'm keeping it. Rosie loves it. She thinks it's your dog."

"I know. Zip thinks the same thing. All he did this afternoon was moon over it. That's why I took him for the walk."

"Rosie didn't eat her supper."

"Zip didn't eat his either. Maybe we could feed them when we get to your house. Together they might eat. Are you agreeable to that?"

"Sure, why not? What else makes a perfect mother?"

The Cajun threw his hands in the air. "I don't know . . . maybe one who doesn't palm her kid off on a housekeeper, one who goes to his baseball games and school plays. One who isn't too busy. One who says I love you once in a while."

"My mother did all that, and she wasn't perfect. No, it has to be more than that." Josie hiccuped again.

"When you find out, please let me know. Whoa, this is where you live. See, the sign says Dupré Catering."

"I knew that. I was going to go in the front way. It's dark going around back. What do you want to do?"

"Let's go in the front. You'll probably kill yourself on that cockamamie walk you have in the back."

He didn't like the ladybugs. She'd get rid of them tomorrow. Every last one.

Josie pushed open the door. "I'm home," she yelled.

"I'm upstairs," Kitty responded.

"Kitty doesn't like unexpected company. She likes to prepare for company."

"I won't stay long. Let's just feed the dogs, and then I'll leave."

"That sounds like a plan," Josie said, flopping down on one of the kitchen chairs. "Do your thing."

The clock read ten-thirty when Josie finished the coffee in front of her. She squeezed her eyes shut as she tried to remember what she had said under the lamppost. She shuddered when she remembered swinging around it. Had she really told him about the diplomat? Of course she had—she always had loose lips when she had too much to drink, which was usually Christmas Eve. One day out of the year she let it get away from her. Now it was two days. She cleared her throat. "Thank you for walking me home."

"It was my pleasure. I can't remember when I've had such an interesting evening. This is a very nice house. Have you lived here all your life?"

"Except when I went away to school, and then Kitty and I lived in Baton Rouge after college until our parents died. We came back here to take over the business. The article said you live here in the Garden District, too."

"I do when I'm not traveling or when I'm at our main headquarters."

"Why did you come here today? Did you want to hire us?"

"I thought I did. Now I'm not sure. Don't look like that. It has nothing to do with you or your business. I'm not sure it's the right thing for me to be doing. I don't normally make rash decisions, and that was a rash decision. It might be a good idea for you to pick up your dog, and I'll carry Zip out to our wagon and take him home."

The boxer reared back and let out an ungodly howl that sent chills up Josie's spine. Rosie started to dance in circles, whining and pawing the floor.

"This is a problem," the Cajun said. "Zip knows the word 'home' and he knows the word 'wagon.' He's not about to go to either. How about if I leave him here tonight and pick him up in the morning. If I walk him now, he'll be good till eight tomorrow morning. I'll come by and pick him up then if that's okay with you."

Josie rubbed her temples. "It doesn't look like I have much of a choice. You're going to have to figure something out. I'm not keeping your dog."

"I'll bring some fresh *beignets*. You make the coffee. Would you like to have dinner with me tomorrow evening?"

Would she? Of course she would. No, she wouldn't. There was no point. Plus he probably just wanted her to keep his dog. No, a thousand times no. "Yes. What time?"

"Seven-thirty. Commander's Palace okay with you?"

"Yes, Commander's Palace is fine with me." She had a date. Kitty was going to be ecstatic. What to wear? She would have to go shopping.

"I really like what you've done with this house. It feels like . . . a home. It's warm and cozy. You know people live here. I like sunlight in the morning."

"I do, too. I think the kitchen and breakfast nook are my favorite rooms in the whole house." Just for a moment she thought she saw the same miserable look in his eyes that she'd seen under the lamppost. Then it was gone.

"I'll walk the dogs. Ten minutes tops."

Josie raced to the downstairs bathroom, where she gargled lustily. She ran a brush through her hair, pinched her cheeks before she ran a lipstick lightly over her lips. She blotted it carefully so it wouldn't look like she'd just put it on. *Why am I doing this?*

"I can see myself out."

"That's all right. I have to lock up anyway. You can leave your wagon here if you like."

"I'll drive over in the morning and put it in the trunk. Thanks for doing this."

He was so close she could smell his minty breath, or was it hers? She wondered what it would be like to lay her head against his chest. "I guess I'll see you for breakfast."

"Eight-fifteen. I'm usually prompt."

"Prompt is good."

She sensed his intent to kiss her. She was about to step backward, but instead she stepped into his arms. Nothing in the world could have prepared her for the feel of his arms, the touch of his lips. Her head spun as her heart hammered in her chest. And then her head was against the hard wall of his chest. It felt as right and wonderful as she knew it would.

"Good night, Josie Dupré."

In a daze, Josie could only nod. She stood in the open doorway until he disappeared in the dark, velvety night.

"I saw everything from the top of the steps," Kitty squealed. "How was it? Do you like him? Is he nice? Did he ask you out? Hurry up, tell me everything. How come his dog is still here?"

"In a word, *spectacular*. Yes to everything, and the dog is staying because he wouldn't leave and he's bringing *beignets* for breakfast as long as we make the coffee. He's taking me to Commander's Palace for dinner tomorrow night. I've never been kissed like that in my life. Never. Ever. He has sad eyes, Kitty. I don't know why that is. I don't think he's that arrogant man the magazine article said he is. He's something totally different. Don't ask me how I know it. I just do. I suspect, and this is just a guess on my part, but I think something happened to him along the way. I asked him what he thought a perfect mother was and his answers blew my mind. It's so strange. Everyone's version of a perfect mother is something totally different. I gotta tell you, though, that was a kiss I won't soon forget."

"Woweee! I hope it all works out for you, Josie. Who knows? This guy might turn out to be Mr. Perfect. We could have a double wedding. Twins are supposed to have double weddings. What could be better?" Kitty said, clapping her hands.

"You can say that again. You lock up, okay? I'm going to bed."

"Sweet dreams, Josie."

"Count on it."

Three

The stainless-steel kitchen of Dupré Catering was fragrant with the rich smell of a slow-baking praline pie. Every burner on the Sub-Zero stove held something equally as fragrant and tantalizing. Kitty was, as Josie put it, cooking up a storm. Hands on her hips, Kitty eyeballed her sister, and said, "Mama is probably spinning in her grave knowing you can't even boil water, Josie. It's not hard. What in the world are you going to do if you get married and your husband expects you to cook dinner for him. Well?" Kitty demanded when her sister stared at her with a blank expression.

"Well?" Kitty prodded.

"I'll hire a cook. It's natural for you. You love to cook and bake. I don't. I can boil eggs and make coffee and toast. I'll never starve as long as I can do that. So, tell me: What did you think of you know who?"

"Charming. He loves his dog. Any man who loves an animal is okay in my book. I'm sorry he left so quickly. I thought you said he was staying for breakfast. Bringing it and setting it on the table is something else. He picked up his dog and took off like the devil himself was on his heels."

"He said something came up. Maybe the two of us intimidated him," Josie said thoughtfully as she moved heavy crockery from one end of the long work counter to the other.

"Nothing can intimidate that man. Trust me. I think women tend to aggravate and frustrate him. I got that from between the lines of the article. I don't think he could compete against a woman. Some men are like that. I know you're going to give him a run for his money. Do you think maybe you could be a little less picky and give the guy a chance? You aren't getting any younger, sister dear. That big number thirty is just months away."

Josie moved the crockery back to the other end of the counter and then rearranged the stainless-steel utensils in a neat line. "So what's all this?" she asked, pointing at the simmering pots.

"Some new things I'm trying out for the Brignacs' Mardi Gras party. You said they wanted something different. I'll bring a sample over later for Rosie to sniff for her seal of approval. If she likes it, we'll go with it. If not, I'll try something else. Whose turn is it to take the food over to the shelter?" Taking their test recipes to the homeless shelter was something they did every day.

"I did it on Friday, so it's your turn. You were coming down with your cold, remember?"

"Yep, I do remember. The pie smells wonderful. Want a piece when it cools off?"

"No, I do not. These hips have all the extra padding they need. I'm going over to the cottage and start to plan Mrs. Lobelia's Mardi Gras party. She just wants the standard stuff. I also want to try to get a couple of my newspaper articles written. If I'm ahead of the game, there won't be as much pressure as last year. I think my first two recipes are going to be the ones you whipped up last week. I particularly like the crabmeat ravigote. It livens up the palate. Then I thought I'd do a robust, gutsy rub of some sort for all kinds of fish. I want to play with the ingredients a bit more. The main thing will be how the fish is cooked. I want it to be robust and sturdy, nothing subtle. If I come up with something, I'll buzz you on the intercom. Did you think about a new cornmeal recipe at all?"

"I'm thinking along the lines of an open-faced Cajun crab pie with a buttered-down cornmeal crust. I'm not sure of the seasonings. I'm going to try out a few later on. It'll look good on the packaging if I can get it to fly. By the way, what are you wearing this evening?"

"Whatever I can find in the closet. I'm not sprucing up if that's what you mean."

"Oh."

"Yes, oh," Josie said as she opened the heavy metal door. "See you later."

Josie looked around the backyard. Was it her imagination, or were the trees greener, the sun brighter? Was the air more fragrant than yesterday? To her eye the sky looked like a turquoise canopy. The birds overhead chittered happily. Did they always do that and she didn't pay attention? Why was she noticing everything today? What was there about today that was special? She'd cleaned off the cottage porch, screwed the planters back into the wall under the windows and loaded them up with the colorful geraniums and petunias. Rosie was cuddling with her new toy and the Beanie Baby Josie had repaired. Maybe that was it. Rosie was over her funk. Next to Kitty, Rosie was the only thing in the world Josie loved.

She had a date tonight but she'd had lots of dates. Nothing special there. It must be Rosie. What else could it be?

The moment Josie sat down at the small secretary, the appointment book open in front of her, the phone rang at the same instant a fax started to come through. She wasn't able to take a deep breath to relax until well past the noon hour, at which point she slammed the appointment book shut and turned on the answering machine. She pressed the intercom button next to the secretary.

"What's up?" Kitty asked in a harried voice.

"I'll tell you what's up. I had to turn on the answering machine. We are booked solid until the end of May. That means we can't take a brunch or even a tea unless we hire more people and even then what good is it going to do us? You can't cook more than you do and there are just so many hours in a day. I hate turning away customers. Do you have any suggestions?"

"We could hire the girl I was telling you about—the one I met when I went back to culinary school for the reunion. She's really good, and she said she hates her job because all they allow her to do is make salads. She'll want big bucks and you said we were in no position to pay out that kind of money. She won't want to give up her job with-out some kind of guarantee. You know how hard it is to get a job in this town."

"Let me run some numbers. I won't rule it out at this point, but if it looks like we'll be paying her most of the new business, what's the point? We might have to raise our prices. We'll still have to pay her during the summer when business is so slow we can barely keep our heads above water. What about a trainee, an apprentice?"

"You get what you pay for, Josie. I don't think either one of us wants to gamble that they won't screw up some-one's dinner party. We have an excellent reputation. Why take a chance?"

"How did Mom and Dad do it? They earned a real nice living doing this, put us through college and had money in the bank and we always took a month's vaca-tion."

"They both cooked. You don't cook, Josie."

The silence on the intercom was something both dreaded. Josie's shoulders slumped. "Talk to you later."

It wasn't like she hadn't tried her hand at cooking. She had. With disastrous results. Kitty had thrown up her hands in disgust on three separate occasions when she'd tried to teach Josie the basic elements. She'd even gone so far as to enroll in a night cooking course in secret. The school had refunded her money after the third class. Everyone wasn't meant to cook. Everyone didn't have the same traits, the same skills. Kitty couldn't add two num-bers together, much less make sense of the computer.

Josie's shoulders slumped even farther. She had to do

something to take the load off Kitty. What? What would her mother have done if she'd been in a similar position? Her gaze traveled to the tiny ledge that ran around the entire room. When they were children the ledge held small toys and decorations. Today it held family photographs. She leaned closer to look into the smiling eyes of her mother. She wished, the way she'd wished a thousand times before, that there was a way to communicate with the woman with the laughing eyes. "I wish you were here, Mom. I really do. We didn't get to say good-bye. There are so many things I need to tell you. God, I used to write you letters by the bushel, but I never gave them to you. Kitty didn't either. Those letters were full of our childish problems, our teenage problems, and then our college problems. At least we perceived them to be problems. Maybe we were smarter than we thought and knew they weren't important, so that's why we never gave them to you. I don't know what to do, Mom. We aren't the business-people you and Dad were. We can't seem to find that perfect niche that makes it all work. Kitty has had one cold after another. She's in that kitchen from sunup to sundown. When she gets married things are really going to be different. I don't know if we can make a go of it."

Josie looked down at the yellow legal pad in front of her. From long years of habit she'd written the letter while saying the words aloud. Tears burned her eyes when she ripped off the yellow sheet from the tablet. She folded it neatly and slid it into a Dupré Catering envelope. She wiped at her eyes with the back of her hand as she made her way through the second room of the cottage to a file cabinet. She sifted through the folders until she found one labeled: *Josie's Letters to Mom*. She removed the rubber bands to slide in her letter. There had to be a hundred, maybe more, in the brown accordion case. Her hand plucked one of the old letters out of the folder. It had been years since she looked at the letters. It hurt too much.

Dear Mom,

You said we are not to act mean and ugly and do bad things. You were mean and ugly to me today when you said my hair looked like the bush by the front door. I did brush it. You forgot to buy that stuff to make my curls soft. Charlie White heard you say that. He made fun of me all day at school. Kitty said I shouldn't cry, so I didn't cry, I don't like you today, Mom. I might like you tomorrow. Kitty said I will. Maybe I won't.

Your daughter Josephine

Josie slid the ruled paper back into the plain white envelope that said "Mom" on the front. She remembered that day so well. That night there had been two bottles of hair conditioner in the bathroom. She'd cried herself to sleep.

Maybe she should burn the letters or put them through the shredder. They still hurt. Had she ever written any nice letters? If so, had she given them to her mother? Why couldn't she remember? "I wish you were here, Mom. I wish that so much. Father Michael said you're always with us in spirit. I have a hard time with that. Maybe if you gave me a sign or did something, I'd understand. I don't know what to do."

She was standing there like a ninny, expecting a response, when she knew there wouldn't be one. Her mother used to say, "Foolish, foolish girl. Why did you do this or that?" Her response had always been the same: "Because I'm me and I wanted to do it."

"Easy, easy, Rosie. What's the matter?" Josie said as she bent over to pick up the panting dog. "Oh, I see. The door blew open. So the papers on my desk blew off and are on the floor. It's okay, baby. I'll clean it up. I sure hope we get that screen door back soon."

Josie dropped to her knees to gather up the papers and folders. The yellow sheet with all her notes. She stretched her neck to look out the diamond-shaped windows. There wasn't even a hint of a breeze. It hit her then. The idea that just might solve her problems. Marie Lobelia. How strange that her note page had been on the top stack on her desk. When they blew off, the odds were it would be last in the mess. Instead it lay front and center on the floor, the others scattered to the four corners. *Her mother?*

Coincidence. She absolutely would not pay attention to the tremor in her arms and legs. She wasn't going to think about this or mention it to Kitty. Never in a million years. "C'mon, Rosie, want to go for a ride to the French Quarter? Just let me copy down the phone number and the address. Yes, you can bring Zip's clone with you. Okay, let's go."

Josie buzzed the test kitchen on the intercom. "I'm going to town. Do you want me to fetch anything back?"

"Stop at the music store and see if that new Corinda Carford CD is in yet. I think it's called *Mr. Sandman.*"

Josie loved the *Vieux Carré,* as did most New Orleanians. She liked the idea that the residential district shared streets with shops, restaurants, and other offices. She always felt so alive with the sights and sounds and the odors of the major port city and entertainment hub. She sniffed appreciatively. From living in New Orleans most of her life, she knew that behind the magnificent wrought-iron gates of its buildings were tranquil, intimate courtyards hidden from view, and that Marie Lobelia lived behind one of them. She closed her eyes for a moment, trying to envision the older woman's courtyard. She knew it would be beautiful, as beautiful as the aristocratic lady herself.

Josie parked the car, reached for the Maltese and the slip of paper containing Marie Lobelia's address. Her gaze raked the house numbers. She had a block and a half to go. Rosie squirmed until she was comfortable and proceeded to lick Josie's ear. Josie laughed all the way to the Lobelia gate, where she rang the bell and waited patiently for it to be opened.

"Miss Dupré! How nice of you to visit. Please, come in."

"Mrs. Lobelia, this is so beautiful. Can we sit out here? It's wonderfully cool and shady."

"I think this is my most favorite spot on earth. This

building was the first thing my daddy bought when he became a man. It's been in the family forever. I moved back here fifteen years ago. Can I offer you some refreshment? Perhaps some sweet tea, a cola, or something with a little more gusto. Like a beer perhaps."

"Sweet tea would be wonderful."

"My girl has gone to the market. I'll fetch it for you. Make yourself comfortable. You can put your dog down— she won't be able to get out."

Josie stared with open mouth at the magnificent oak tree in the center of the courtyard. *Barbe espagnol,* also known as Spanish moss, dripped from the branches. The tree had to be three hundred years old. She tried to guess the measurements of the humongous trunk but had to give up. It would take at least four grown men with long arms to reach around it. A wrought-iron bench circled the tree. She knew it was custom-made, for there were no breaks anywhere in the iron. *Amazing,* she thought. Everywhere she looked there were colorful flowers in clay pots on the beautiful, low brick walls. Just the right height for watering. The brick on the ground was just as beautiful, with emerald green moss growing between the bricks, some of which were being pushed askew by the heavy, thick roots of the ancient tree. It didn't alter the beauty of the courtyard one tiny bit. She slipped off her shoes and wiggled her toes over the luscious moss while Rosie sniffed out every nook and cranny. She was careful not to disturb the moss. Moss was precious to New Orleanians.

Josie chose a small wrought-iron bench with a cushion as colorful as the flowers on the walls to sit down on.

Rosie immediately scampered to her side. *I could go to sleep right here,* she thought. *Did Mrs. Lobelia's children play out here when they were children?* Somehow she knew they climbed the old tree and swung from its gnarled old branches. That's what she would have done.

"Here you are, my dear. So, how do you like my courtyard?"

"It's so beautiful I don't know what to say. This tree is so gorgeous, it takes my breath away. Did your children climb it when they were little?"

"Yes they did. I did, too, as a matter of fact. Sometimes I think it cries for children. I talk to it, you know. And to my flowers. I play music for them. I'm not off my rocker, as you young people say. There's a little fountain in the back part by the little grotto, but it isn't working today. We need to replace some hoses. It's so hard to find help these days. It's a little job, and no one wants to spend the time or the effort on little jobs. All they think about is money and how much they can gouge you for. Now, tell me: What brings you here and what can I do for you? Don't tell me you came up with a recipe already."

"I'm good but not that good, Mrs. Lobelia. Actually I came here to make a proposition."

"I'd like it if you would call me Marie and, if it's all right with you, I'll call you Josie. What kind of proposition?"

"The ladies you're inviting to your King Cake party, and the ones you plan to surprise on Mother's Day, are they all of an age with you, retired so to speak?"

"Yes, they are. Why?"

"Are any of them good cooks?"

"Every single one of them is an excellent cook. They fight and squabble over recipes all the time. We spend a lot of time talking about the old days." The tiny, sculpted face registered total horror when she said, "Today we ate Uncle Ben's Rice Bowls. We got them in the freezer at the grocery store. It's so disgusting, I'm ashamed to admit we not only bought them—we ate them, too. You just throw the bowl away. No cleanup. No cleanup allows for more time to watch the soaps. Today it was all suds," she quipped. "I welcome your visit."

"I need some good cooks. I'm afraid I've overextended myself. My sister is wearing herself out. Like you said, it's hard to find good help. I was thinking if some of your relatives and friends could give a few hours a day it would be wonderful. I have a van, so I could drive over here to pick everyone up and then bring them home. Cooking would be mostly late afternoon. I'll pay whatever they want."

"Pay! I can tell you right now none of them will take a penny. What they will do is trample both of us when I tell them. Take Réné for example. She's an expert on Andouille. She has recipes you never dreamed of. Some of them are over a hundred years old, handed down through her family. She is the absolute best. Yvette is a master of jambalaya. She has recipes that have never gone beyond her family. Charlet is our gumbo specialist. They were all wonderful cooks in their day. As long as it doesn't matter if their hands shake or they forget things, they'll certainly agree to help you out."

"That makes me feel a little better. I'll snap them up right now. What's your speciality, Marie?"

"Why do you think I bought the rice bowls? I was never a cook. Everything I ever cooked tasted the same. Bland, no matter how much spice or seasoning I put in things. I was very good at running my father's business, though. When the children were little we had all kinds of help: a cook, a laundress, someone to clean, someone to care for the children. I never had to learn. The truth is, I hate the kitchen."

"You sound like me. I even took cooking lessons. They gave me back my money. We have two parties this Saturday. A late-afternoon one with the food served at four o'clock and a dinner party served at eight o'clock. Is that too soon? I can leave a copy of the menu with you. Aren't you working today, Marie?"

"I just go into the office a few hours early in the morning. I need to be here with my friends. Some of them aren't as . . . spry as the others. The business runs itself more or less. It's so hard to accept that you've been forgotten by those you love with all your heart. I have not seen my son in five years. He calls every few months to say hello. He called yesterday. The last time he called was a week before Christmas. I can't stand the thought that he fits me into his schedule. Maybe I am a foolish old woman, but I don't care. Every time I hear his voice my heart breaks a little more. It's much too painful. Enough of my meandering here. Is there a young man in your life, chère?"

"No, not really. My sister tells me I'm too picky.

Maybe I want bells and whistles. When I give my heart to someone it's going to be forever. My mom gave my dad her heart. She told me once that she said those very words on their wedding day. She said, 'I give you my heart forever and ever.' I was little when she told me that, but it stayed with me. I do have a date tonight. We're going to dinner at Commander's Palace. I can't believe I agreed to go out with someone with a ponytail. I met him when he came to hire us and his dog is the one who created that mess at the cottage. Then I met him again last night when I was walking my dog. He ended up walking me home. Our dogs are smitten with each other."

"It sounds like the beginning of one of those romance novels. A bad one," Marie said. "What else does he have going for him?"

"I think he might be rich. He travels a lot. He seems to love his dog. Good dresser, and he has a real nice body. He's probably one of those love 'em and leave 'em types. I have no time for that. I don't even know why I said yes. Probably because of the dogs. Oh, I forgot to tell you: He left the dog with me last night. I'm starting to get nervous thinking about all this. I know where he lives. I could stop by and cancel."

"Good Lord, chère, why would you want to do that? You go out and have a good time. From the looks of you I don't think there are too many women who can hold a candle to you. You are a beautiful young woman. Strut your stuff. Make him dance to your tune. And don't baby-sit his dog again either!"

"Yes, ma'am," Josie said, saluting smartly.

"Would you like to meet the ladies before you leave?"

"Absolutely."

Marie put her fingers to her mouth and let loose with an earsplitting whistle. "That'll bring them on the run. Bet you can't do that!"

"Wanna bet! Kitty and I used to try to outwhistle each other. I always won. Listen to this!"

Marie clapped her hands over her ears. "That was good. Really good. Ah, here they are."

They were all shapes and sizes, and all of them wore wide smiles. Like Marie, they wore colorful outfits and pounds of jewelry. In rapid-fire French, with the aid of her hands, Marie Lobelia outlined Josie's request. She ended by saying, *"Laissez les bons temps rouler."*

Josie burst out laughing. "Yes, let the good times roll. I'll be back tomorrow to pick you up around one o'clock. Will that interfere with your soap operas?"

"Not at all."

"Then I'll see you tomorrow. Be sure to lock the gate after me."

Josie picked up Rosie and smiled all the way back to the car. She was still smiling when she parked the Explorer in the driveway. Maybe the good times really would roll. Now she had to tell Kitty what she had done. She crossed her fingers that her sister would approve.

"That's great!" Kitty crowed when Josie told her the news. "No, it's better than great! I can learn from them. God, Josie, think of all those priceless recipes handed down within each family and never given out. I think that's probably the best idea you've ever had. Congratulations!"

"On that thought, I'll leave you. I need to find something to wear tonight. How'd that praline pie come out?"

"Perfect. I made one of those crabmeat pies with the cornmeal. It's good, but something's missing. Take a bite and see if you can tell what it needs."

"Ooohhh, this is good, Kitty. Maybe more salt. No spices. It's more than flavorful. Crusty French bread, a crisp garden salad, and a good bottle of wine. Perfect light supper or a great lunch. A good addition to a brunch, too. I don't think it needs anything. But then what do I know? You can try it on the ladies tomorrow. They'll be your real test. Cut me a sliver for Rosie to sniff."

"What are you going to wear?" Kitty asked, cutting a thick slice of pie that she wrapped in a napkin before she slid the pie into the refrigerator.

"I don't have a clue. That ponytail bothers me."

"You can always cancel. We have the phone number as well as the address."

"I know. It is the last minute. I hate it when someone cancels on me at the last minute. It's just one dinner date. I don't have to see him again if I don't want to."

"What exactly does he do? Do you know? The article just said he had many businesses."

"I don't know but if you really want to know, I'll ask him tonight. Maybe the long black sheath with pearls."

"Boring," Kitty said, rolling her eyes.

"How about the brown linen with the chunky gold belt?"

"You look drab in brown. If you had a tan, it would be different. What about that gauzy green number you wore a few weeks ago? It came back from the cleaners on Monday. If you wear those sexy, strappy heels, you're good to go."

"Okay, sounds good."

"Brush your hair back and wear that gold headband. The one with the matching earrings. If you brush it back, you won't look so young and girlish. You want to look sophisticated."

"Why all the advice, Kitty? You didn't do this when I went out with Mark or any of those other guys whose names I can't remember."

"That's because I knew they were strictly one-nighters. This guy is different, trust me."

"Oh yeah."

"Yeah." Kitty grinned. "Go on, I have some recipes I have to write up. I'm staying at Harry's tonight, so lock up when you get home, okay?"

"No problem. Tell Harry I said hi."

"Will do."

Josie was more nervous than a cat in a rainstorm. How could one date reduce her to this state? "Oh, Mom, I wish you were here. You'd know the answer. You'd say just the right thing, and I'd calm down. I did a bubble bath, washed my hair, shaved my legs. Don't ask me why. I'm wearing a great outfit, sexy shoes, lacy underwear—not that it matters—and I look good. My perfume is supposed to reduce men to blithering idiots. All of that should put me in control. I should feel confident and . . . vital. I'm a jumble of nerves. What will I talk about? First dates are so . . . stressful. What if I can't keep up my end of the conversation? He's got long hair, Mom. You know me, I blurt. I know I'm going to put my foot in it. God, I wish you were here," Josie muttered as she sat down on the edge of the bed. From somewhere faraway, she heard the words to a song she recognized, "You are so beautiful." Kitty must have come in and put the stereo on. She stood up, her legs shaking as she walked to the window. The lights were still on in the test kitchen. That mean Kitty wasn't in the house. She whirled around and swore she smelled her mother's lily of the valley cologne. A wave of dizziness washed over her. No music wafted up the long staircase. "Mom? It's you, isn't it?" She swiveled around and almost turned her ankle in the spike-heeled shoes. Her room looked the same, and it was just as quiet as before. Why would her mother's spirit contact her now? Why now after all this time? Suddenly she wanted to cry, but if she cried, her mascara would run in black streaks down her cheeks. She glanced at her watch. Her imagination was working overtime. Time to go downstairs.

He was prompt. She had to give him that. But then weren't businessmen usually prompt? She smiled a greeting, and suddenly everything felt right. Was it the approving look in his eye, or was it Rosie hovering about his ankles? Zip's guardian. She watched as Paul bent down to pick up the little dog, who sniffed him furiously.

He grinned, showing glistening white teeth. "That's so Zip will know I've seen his *amoureuse.*"

Josie smiled indulgently. "She's never faraway from his likeness. She seems to prefer it to her Beanie Baby. Until you and your dog came along, she was never without it."

"Zip has lost all his zip. He just moons around. I took him with me today, and he didn't even want to get out of the car. The same car he tore to shreds. By the way, that's the car we'll be driving in. I more or less trimmed the strips. It will have to go into the shop for repairs tomorrow. I hope you don't mind riding in it. I put towels on the seats."

"Not at all. I'm ready if you are."

"I can't tell you how I've been looking forward to this all day."

Josie felt her chest puff up. Nothing shy about this guy.

"I used to go to the Commander's Palace all the time when Paul Prudhomme headed up the kitchen. He served this wonderful trout with pecans. I've never tasted anything like it or half as good. I hope you won't be disappointed."

Josie's chest unpuffed. He was talking about fish and nuts, not her. She was tempted to offer up a surly remark, but bit her tongue instead. "I have an excellent recipe for trout and pecans that's all my own. We serve it with red grapes and a sweet vinaigrette. It won a prize."

"Perhaps you'll make it for me someday. You must be

a very good cook to get the centerfold of *Gourmet Party.* Are you really so busy you're turning business away?"

Damn. Now she was flustered. She could feel her neck and face heating up. If ever there was a time to tell him she couldn't cook, this was that time. "Yes, we're very busy. I have a waiting list if any cancellations come through. But then it's always busy when it's time for Mardi Gras. Then Easter and Mother's Day are right around the corner. July and August are slow as a rule; then things pick up after Labor Day. You know what they say: feast or famine. By the way, you didn't say, what it is you do."

"I manage my companies."

"What kind of companies?"

"We have a chain of fast-food restaurants that serve only Cajun food. We package Cajun spices. Just in the South and here in New Orleans. We have a meat-packing plant. I more or less inherited the businesses when my father died. Eldest son, only son kind of thing. We have another chain of restaurants in the North. Again, fast food, but only deep-fried fish and chips. They do very well. I'm constantly on the lookout for new recipes. We run contests from time to time for new recipes."

"And you have no Cajun accent," Josie said.

"I worked really hard to get rid of it. At the time it seemed like the right thing to do if I wanted to fit in. Later, I was sorry."

"It must have been hard on you to deny your heritage. I don't think I could do that."

"I denied a lot of things back then. Unfortunately, you can't unring the bell. Everything in life is a learning experience. Sometimes things just can't be made right."

"I don't believe that for one minute," Josie bristled. "Everyone makes mistakes. I don't think the person has been born who hasn't made a mistake. Besides, everyone deserves a second chance. However, if you fluff the second chance, then you deserve whatever you get."

"And on that profound statement, I believe we will turn this car over to the valet and see what kind of gourmet food we can sink our teeth into. By the way, how were the *beignets* this morning?"

"Stale."

He laughed. "We can try it again tomorrow."

"Why not?"

"Then we have a date for breakfast. Can I bring Zip?"

"Absolutely." *Oh, you fool. He's going to palm the dog off on you for the day. I just know it.*

"You're a good sport, Josie Dupré," Paul said, holding the car door for her. His gaze lingered on the long expanse of her silky leg.

So he's a leg man. "My mother taught us always to be good sports even if we had to grit out teeth while we were being sporting."

He laughed again.

She loved the sound. Loved it, loved it, loved it. The ponytail had to go. She didn't mean to give voice to her thought and was shocked senseless when the words tumbled from her mouth. "Why do you wear a ponytail?"

"Because I like it. My hair is curlier than yours. When I smooth it back, it's straight. Does it offend you?"

"I don't know. I've never gone out with a man whose hair was longer than mine."

"There's a first time for everything."

"Yes, there is," Josie said smartly.

"I like your honesty. Is that something else your mother taught you?"

"Yes. And to take responsibility for my own actions. I don't know why it is, but lately I've been thinking a lot about my mother. You would have liked her. She had the prettiest smile, and she had this one pink dress that was so beautiful. She looked like a movie star in it. She had a little pink hat with a flower on it. She always wore it to church on Sunday. You could always tell which room she was in because it smelled like lilies of the valley. It wasn't overpowering or anything like that. It was sweet and clean like she was. I'm sorry. I didn't meant to rattle on like that."

"It's all right."

But it wasn't all right. She knew somehow she'd struck a wrong nerve. Like he said, you couldn't unring the bell. "I'm hungry," she blurted.

"Then I suggest we eat." His touch sent electric currents up her arm when he cupped her elbow in his hand to lead her into the restaurant.

Four

"I don't know about you, Josie, but I need to walk that dinner off. How about a walk down Bourbon Street? The trick will be to find a parking space. Are you up for it?"

"I'd love to walk it. I guess your dinner was all you expected. Was your trout as good as you remembered when Prudhomme was the chef?"

"Not quite, but still good. Sometimes the memories are like anticipation: better left alone."

There was such sadness in Paul's voice, and Josie's head jerked upright. "I'm game for Bourbon Street," she said lightly.

"Good. We'll stop for a nightcap. Have you been to Preservation Hall lately?"

"Not for years and years. My mother frowned on Bourbon Street and what she called the sinful atmosphere. I do love jazz and blues, though. Kitty and I used to sneak down when we'd come home from college. Do you know who's there tonight?"

"Percy Humphrey, Harold Dejan, and the Olympia Brass Band. I saw it in the paper this week. I haven't been there for a while myself."

"Do they still have those hard wooden chairs and the mildewed cushions on the floor?" Josie asked as she held out her hand to feel the first raindrops of the evening.

"It's still as run-down as ever, but it is a landmark. I think of it as a rustic environment. Do you want to change your mind since it's starting to rain?"

"No. I have to warn you: My hair will spread out like a fire bush. When it rains I need a hat."

"We can fix that. We'll buy you a hat!"

"That's the best offer I've had all day," Josie retorted. "If we have time, I'd like to stop at this other club my sister loves: Port Orleans, 228 Bourbon Street. Kitty and Harry are friends of the band. She says they are the greatest, and she doesn't impress easily; nor does Harry. The band is called Butterfunck. Johnny Pappas on guitar and lead vocals, Réné Richard on bass, and Trey Crain on drums. She said she would kill to look like Johnny's girl, Jeanne Boudreaux. So, we need to check her out, too. She raves about them all the time. I'd like to see them. Do you mind?"

"It will be my pleasure to take you there wearing your new hat."

"You are too kind, sir." Josie giggled. "Ah, I see a parking space. Hurry up and grab it!"

"You are aggressive, aren't you?" Paul said, as he expertly maneuvered the big Mercedes into the spot.

"I don't think we'll have to worry about anyone stealing this car when they see the inside." Josie giggled again.

"It's raining harder. Are you going to be able to walk in those shoes?"

"No, these shoes are for standing around in or sitting down. I'll carry them and go barefoot. This is the Big Easy and Bourbon Street. Anything goes—you know that."

"Then let's do it!" Paul reached for her hand, and they sprinted off. He stopped for a minute and pulled her close to him. "This is the most amazing street in the world. Just look at it! Look at the people. You can literally smell the street and it *never* leaves you. You can be ten thousand miles away, and if you close your eyes, you can see and smell and hear everything that goes on. This is what I remember when I think of New Orleans. I've always loved the French Quarter, the Garden District, the French Market, and Bourbon Street. Did you ever attend Mardi Gras?"

"Sad to say, no."

"Here we go," Paul said, pulling her into the first shop, which was like a dozen other shops along the way. Within seconds she was wearing a baseball cap that said BOURBON STREET. She giggled when Paul plopped one on his own head. He looked cute in his custom-made suit and baseball cap, the ponytail sticking out the back. She reached for the feathered mask and the strands of beads he handed her—Mardi Gras beads. "Your neck will turn green and red but what the hell! This is Bourbon Street, and no visit is a real visit unless you buy a mask and the beads. Okay, let's go. Run!"

They were soaked to the skin when they reached Preservation Hall. Paul handed over the admission money and was told, "Standing room only, sir." He looked questioningly at Josie, who shrugged and nodded.

Josie pointed to a sign over the musicians' heads. She whispered, "You have to pay extra for them to play 'When the Saints Go Marching In.' It doesn't say how much."

Paul reached into his pocket as he walked over to the cashier and spoke quietly. She heard him say, "Now, when this set is done." *Money talks,* Josie mused.

Josie almost swallowed her tongue when Percy Humphrey stood up and said, "And now for the little lady with the baseball cap and curly hair, we are going to play 'When The Saints Go Marching In.' Hit it, boys!"

Josie's cheeks flamed. "I can't believe you did that!" The old building literally shook with the thunder of the small crowd who stomped, sang, whistled, and clapped; Josie's voice was the loudest.

As they dashed through the rain, Josie said, "That was so wonderful. Thank you. I can't wait to tell Kitty. Thank you for bringing me here."

"My pleasure. I'm afraid your dress is ruined. I seem to have a knack for messing you up."

"This old thing!" Josie said, indicating the dress she'd paid a small fortune for. "Don't give it another thought. By the way, why are we running? We're already soaking wet."

"You have a point." Paul slowed his long-legged stride to match her shorter one. He reached for her hand as they plodded through the puddles.

Josie felt absolutely giddy with his touch.

Music blasted from open doorways as they walked along, people with umbrellas jostling each other, the drinks in their hands spilling into the puddles at their feet. Laughter rocked the street. "There will be a hundred thousand people on this street in a few weeks for Mardi Gras," Josie said happily. "With the exception of Times Square on New Year's Eve, I can't think of a single place with a crowd to match it. I think you were right about these Mardi Gras beads—my dress is turning all different colors."

Paul threw back his head and laughed. And right then, in the blink of an eye, Josie Dupré fell in love with Paul Brouillette.

"Six strands of beads for ninety-nine cents. What do you expect?" He laughed again.

Josie blinked. Did he realize she was falling in love with him? What was he feeling, if anything? He looked at her then and smiled. She smiled back. He squeezed her hand. She squeezed his hand.

"I think this is the place," Paul said as he ushered Josie into the bar. His head snapped to attention when the small band began a new set of tunes. "They're loud. I might be a little too old for this," he said, helping her onto a high barstool. "What will you have to drink?"

"Beer's good. I'm still full from dinner. Kitty says we have to ask them to play 'Mustang Sally.'"

Paul shrugged out of his jacket and placed it around her shivering shoulders. "Two Buds," he said to the hovering waitress. "I can't hear myself," he shouted.

"You aren't supposed to hear yourself. You're supposed to listen. They must be good; the place is crowded. I like them," Josie said, banging the ashtray on the table in time with the music. Paul fished in his pocket and walked over to the band, where he mouthed the words, "Play 'Mustang Sally.'" She watched as money changed hands.

They stayed until the band, went on break. The moment Josie yawned, Paul lifted her off the barstool and ushered her out the door. "We'll come back for Mardi Gras if I'm in town."

Josie stepped in a puddle and yelped. "Okay," he said, picking her up and slinging her over his shoulder. "It's time to go home. It's been a very interesting evening."

"It's always interesting when you fall in love," Josie mumbled as she bounced around on Paul's shoulders.

Paul grinned as rain beat down on him and the slender girl on his shoulder. "I'm going to run now, so hold on."

My rear end is right in his face, Josie realized. Suddenly her head jerked upright, the baseball cap landing in a puddle. What if he heard what she'd just mumbled. "Hey, slow down! Stop! My hat fell off. I want the hat! Put me down."

A devil perched itself on Paul's shoulder as he swung around, searching under the garish neon light for the biggest puddle he could find. He swung around again and dropped her, rear end first, into an ankle-deep puddle.

Josie winced with the jolt to her posterior but was quick enough to reach out with her right hand to grasp Paul's ankle. He went down on all fours as rain pelted the two of them. Josie crawled away, laughter bubbling in her throat as her hand snaked out for the baseball cap that was now soaking wet. She plopped it on her head.

People hurrying to get to their cars joined their laughter as they passed by. No one stopped. This was, after all, the Big Easy, where *laissez les bons temp rouler* was the rule of the day. "My mother would never approve of this. What about your mother?" Josie managed to gasp as peals of laughter rocked her shoulders. "You look pretty silly, sitting there in that puddle. Your suit is ruined. My dress is ruined. Just like your car. Everything is ruined. Isn't that funny?"

The moment was gone as fast as it arrived. Paul was on his feet, his hand stretched out to help her up. "I guess I did look rather silly, and my mother wouldn't care. It's late. I need to think about getting you home."

"Wait a minute. Why the switch up? What did I say to put that look on your face? That you look silly? You did look silly, as silly as I looked. Hey, we're on Bourbon Street. It was a silly moment. It was fun. Now you look and act and sound like a . . . stuffy banker. I guess it is time to go home," she said, all the fun gone from her voice.

Later, in her driveway, Paul turned to her and said, "For some reason you rattle me. I don't understand it. I'm sorry if I took all the fun out of your evening there at the end."

"You rattle me, too. Did I do something, say something?"

"No. It was just the end of a very long day. Do you still want me to stop by with breakfast?"

"I'd like that."

"Then it's a date." He made a move to open the door. She stopped him.

"Don't get out. I'll go around the back. I want to take off these wet clothes in the laundry room. I can't believe it's still raining. Thanks for the beads and stuff. I really enjoyed the evening. I'll see you in the morning."

"Good night, Josie."

She'd really thought he was going to reach for her and kiss her good night. Instead, he gave her a jaunty little salute before he backed his car out of the driveway. Damn, maybe she wasn't in love after all. Then what was that giddy feeling that ripped through her back there in the rain?

Josie sloshed through the rain in the dark. She wished she'd had the good sense to turn on the back light before she left the house. It didn't matter—she knew the yard and garden by heart. She stopped in her tracks when she heard a sound coming from the back porch—a sound that literally stopped her heart. She waited, aware that the tiny purse on her shoulder would be no weapon against an intruder. There was a broom on the back porch. If she could get to the back porch, it might help. If not, it was her time to get mugged. Whoever he was, he was a heavy breather. Chills ran up and down her spine. "I have a gun!" she squeaked. "I'm going to shoot and if I hit you . . . Oh my God," she yelled when a monstrous four-legged creature slammed up against her, knocking her to the ground. "Zip! How did you get here?" She groaned. "Stop licking me. I don't need a bath. I've been in the rain all night. Okay, okay, come on. I'll let you in. Poor thing, you're soaked, too. Have you been here *all* night? This is amazing. How ever did you get out? Your owner is going to be worried sick just the way I would be if Rosie got out."

The boxer ran up the steps and stood panting by the back door, his impatience showing by the way he pranced and danced around the porch as Josie fumbled with the key. She watched for a minute as both dogs tussled on the kitchen floor, their delight in one another a joy to experience. "This," she muttered, "must be true love.

"Hey, Rosie, it's me. You know, me. Your owner. I'm the one who feeds and walks you and makes sure you don't get fleas." The little dog tilted her head, barked twice, her tail swishing furiously. "Okay, if that's all the greeting I get, I guess it's okay. Go on. Keep on doing whatever it is you were doing. I let this guy in, you know."

She was down to her skimpy, lacy underwear when the phone in the kitchen rang. She padded over to the counter and picked up the phone. "He's here. He was waiting on the back porch. Right now he's under my kitchen table. You were already out of the driveway when I found him."

"How did you know it was me on the phone?" Paul asked, a smile in his voice.

"I don't know anyone else who would call me at one o'clock in the morning. Let's just say it was an educated guess. It's okay if he stays. You can pick him up in the morning."

"He knows how to open the French doors. I didn't know that until this evening. He's never done anything like that before. It's amazing that he found his way to your house and that he's safe and sound. I guess I'll have to crate him from now on when I leave. I hate doing that to him. I wouldn't want to be put in a cage, would you?"

"No, I wouldn't. He's fine. I'll see you in the morning."

"You're a good sport, Josie. Thank you."

Good sport. No kiss good night. Stuffy-banker attitude. "You're welcome."

"I'll make sure the *beignets* are fresh this time. See you in the morning. Thanks again for agreeing to keep Zip."

The clock on the nightstand shrilled to life. Josie cracked an eyelid. She groaned. No one should have to get up at five-thirty in the morning. Absolutely no one. She swung her legs over the side of the bed and groaned again. The boxer rose to his feet and stretched. Rosie did the same thing. "Time to go out, huh? Okay, let's go and let's make it quick. We have company coming for breakfast." She leaned over the boxer. "Your owner is coming for you." The dog stared at her for a long minute before he dropped to his belly and squirmed his way under her bed.

Rosie yipped her disapproval by peering under the bed; Josie dropped to the floor. "Look, Zip. Maybe I'm wrong and your owner *isn't* coming. Maybe it's wishful thinking on my part. I'm going to pick up your girlfriend and take her outside. If you pee under my bed, you will never be allowed up here again. I know you understand everything I'm saying, so let's hop to it." The huge dog dropped his head between his paws and stared at her. It was obvious he had no intention of moving.

Josie whirled around to grab Rosie before she could belly under the bed to join Zip. They were back in the house in under ten minutes. Zip was still under the bed. "If you're under there for the long haul, we're going to have a problem," Josie said as she headed for the bathroom.

It was six forty-five when Josie exited the bathroom dressed in a swirling lavender skirt with matching blouse. "Let's go downstairs where I'll have some *café noir* and you get some kibble. That's an order, Rosie." She wasn't the least bit surprised when neither dog followed her down the stairs and out to the kitchen. Rosie was always ahead of her and would jump up on one of the chairs to wait expectantly for either a treat or some real food. The sudden urge to cry was so strong, she bit down on her lower lip. Damn, her well-ordered life was suddenly upside down. "I wish you were here, Mom. Something's happening to me, and I'm not sure how I should deal with it. If you were here, you'd know exactly what to say to me. It's really strange, Mom, that Rosie would choose the chair you always used to sit on when we had our *café noir*. You always said our early-morning coffee was the best. I put chicory in it just like you used to do. Rosie is like a person. She really is. Damn it, I just want to cry."

"Then goddamn it, cry!" Kitty said from the open doorway. "You talking to Mom again? I talked to her myself last night. You know, to apologize for running buck-ass naked through the rain, slurping on a mango. Just in case she could, you know, kind of *see*. Why do you want to cry?"

"Because Rosie doesn't need me anymore. All she wants is Zip. They're both under my bed, and Zip won't come out because I told him Paul was coming for him. When I got home last night he was waiting on the back porch. Paul said he knows how to open the French doors. He came here. He must have been here for hours. I felt sorry for him, so I let him stay. Paul's bringing *beignets,* and I just made coffee. Tell me, what was it like?"

"You mean being *naked* in the rain or the part about the mango or the details on how it felt being chased by Harry? Mangos are so juicy, especially if they're ripe. Harry loved licking the juice off my body. In a word, *spectacular*! That's with a capital S."

"I see now why you were talking to Mom." Josie laughed. "Set the table."

"Paper plates okay?"

"Sure. I'm too busy today to do any cleanup. The ladies are coming to help. This little luncheon we're catering and the dinner party will be a good way for them to dive in and see how it all works. I hope for all our sakes that it works out."

"Me too. If it does, we might be able to take that ski trip in December. All we do is work, Josie. I didn't realize how tired I was until last night when I let it all hang out. I really didn't want to get dressed and come here this morning. I'm going to be such a good wife to Harry."

"The best," Josie said with a catch in her voice. Everyone was leaving her. First her mother and dad, then Rosie, and now Kitty. She would be alone with a lovesick dog.

"I can't wait to get married and have kids. Lots and lots of kids. I wonder if I'll have twins. That would be so wonderful. Harry told me last night he might get transferred to Atlanta. I didn't want to tell you, but you need to know."

"Georgia! When?"

"Six weeks. I'm not going to go with him. I'll finish out the year and move after we get married. Harry said he would come back every weekend. I don't know how that's going to work out since our busiest times are the weekends."

"You love him very much, don't you, Kitty?"

"With all my heart and soul."

"Then you have nothing to worry about. Everything will work out just fine. I know you're worried about me, and that's not good. I'll be fine. The worst-case scenario is we sell off the business and I go back to Baton Rouge. Trust me when I tell you it will not be a punishment. I love Baton Rouge."

"I hear a car."

"That means our breakfast is here."

"Do you want me to leave?"

"Absolutely not. Sit down. I'll get the door. Don't ask him any questions," she hissed over her shoulder.

"Okay," Kitty hissed back.

"Beautiful day, isn't it?" Paul said as he handed over a bakery box and followed Josie back to the breakfast nook. "Where's Zip?" he asked, looking around.

He looked so good. He smelled even better. She thought about the suit he'd been wearing the previous night and wondered if it was salvageable. She shrugged. "He's under my bed with Rosie, and he won't come out. I made the mistake of telling him you were coming to get him. I'm sorry. He simply won't come out."

"You need to be stern. There's a certain tone of voice you have to use. You have to show animals you're their superior, their boss, if you will. Special treats or people food usually work. If none of that works, then you have to trick them. Do you have any ham or cheese?"

Josie opened the refrigerator and cut off a chunk of cheese. "It's not going to work. I think you're going to have to take the bed apart."

"That's rather extreme, don't you think? By the way, I have to go to New York today. I'm going to drop Zip off at a dog spa. He's been there before, and he actually likes it. Can I give them your name in case anything goes awry? Just in case he gets sick, which I don't think he will. He's healthy as a horse and has had all his shots. A friend of mine used to look in on him when I boarded him, but he's in Europe."

No. I'm not a dog-sitter. I'm going to be busy. I think I'm starting to get your schtick, Mr. Brouillette. A dog is a responsibility, and if you aren't willing to take that respon-

sibility, then you don't deserve to have that dog. I'm not agreeing to any such thing. Find some other sucker.

"I'll only be gone a week. Ten days at the most."

"You're leaving your dog for *ten* whole days!"

"I don't have any other choice. Can I give them your phone number?"

"Yes." *Fool,* her mind shrieked. Josie looked up to see her sister clamp her hand over her mouth to keep from laughing.

"Okay, boy, let's go. Time to come out. Don't make me come in there after you," Paul said as he crouched down to peer under the bed.

Rosie's little head poked out. She snarled and lunged at Paul's hand. He snatched it back so quickly that Josie burst out laughing. "I think she's trying to tell you not to mess with her man."

"Now, Zip. I'm going to count to three! One! Two! Three!"

"No one seems to be moving." Josie giggled again.

"I see that. All right, we'll take the mattress and box spring off. How'd he get under there anyway?"

"He crawled on his belly."

"I'll take this end. You and your sister take the other end. That way, we'll just have to tilt the box spring."

Five minutes later, just as they all moved in sync to lift the box spring, Zip and Rosie hopped over the frame and raced for the hall and the stairs.

"Damn it, I have a plane to catch. Can they get out?"

"I don't think so," Josie said, straightening the box

spring with Kitty's help. They gave the mattress a shove. It landed squarely on top of the box spring. Both girls dusted their hands dramatically.

"This is just a wild thought, but five will get you ten you end up taking care of that dog," Kitty said. "Sounds like a war going on down there. Maybe we should check it out."

"Maybe we should," Josie said, eyeing the wrinkled sheets that had come untucked. "I haven't even had my coffee yet."

"You're in love with him, aren't you?" Kitty said, taking her sister's arm and pulling her around to face her. "It's okay if you are, Josie. Remember how Mom set eyes on Dad and they were married three weeks later? It happens like that sometime. Roll with it."

"I don't know about the love part, but I do feel a very strong attraction to him. He's so different from the men I've dated. He didn't even kiss me last night. There's something out of whack about him. One minute he's up and the next he closes up. I'm starting to think maybe I said the wrong thing, gave off bad vibes. You know me."

Kitty wrapped her arm around her sister's shoulders. "What will be will be. Enjoy whatever it is you have right now. Open up, Josie."

Josie nodded. "Let's go downstairs and see if he's made any progress."

"You a bettin' woman, Josie?"

"Nope. Hey, let's slide down the banister."

Kitty hiked up her long skirt and whooped her pleasure as she slid down the polished teak wood banister.

"Ninety miles an hour—isn't that what Dad said? Wow, when was the last time we did that?"

"The day after . . . after the funeral. It was stupid then, and it's stupid now. We thought it would make us feel better. It didn't."

"Oh. How could I have forgotten that?"

"The same way I did until this moment. You block it out."

Josie walked into the sunny kitchen. Her gaze swept past Paul's helpless expression to the snarling dogs under the table. It was a losing battle—one she wasn't going to win either. She sighed. "It's okay, Rosie. He can stay."

The relief on Paul's face brought a smile to Josie's. A long time ago her mother had said there was nothing in the world she wouldn't do to bring a smile to her father's face. Maybe she was like her mother after all.

"If you leave now, he'll know he's staying. Tell him."

Paul dropped to his haunches. "Okay, big guy, you can stay with Rosie. We're going to talk about this when I get back." Zip bellied out from under the table to lick his master's face. Rosie did a wild dance around the kitchen before Josie opened the back door. Both dogs hit the open doorway at a dead run.

"I don't know how to thank you, Josie. I'm sorry about last night. I had no idea Zip could get out. I'm going to do some hard thinking where he's concerned. I'm sorry about breakfast, too. It was nice seeing you again, Kitty. When I get back I'd like to take you both to Brennan's for breakfast. This is the key to my house in case you need to go there for any of Zip's things. Here's a number where you can reach me if you have to. I'll call to check on him if that's okay with you."

"No problem," Josie said coolly. "You don't have to call. We'll all be just fine. Your dog is having the time of his life," she said, pointing to the backyard, where both dogs were running in circles. "You better hurry or you'll miss your flight." Her voice turned downright frosty.

"The bed . . ."

"We fixed it," Kitty chirped. "Women can do anything men can do."

Paul's eyebrows shot upward. It looked like he was about to say something, but changed his mind.

"You don't want to go there, *Mr.* Brouillette," Josie said.

"Now you're angry with me. You aren't going to take it out on my dog, are you?"

Josie opened the door and motioned him to leave. "Your dog will be just fine."

"That was kind of bitchy wasn't it?" Kitty said quietly.

"Yes, I guess it was," Josie said, her eyes on the dogs in the yard. How happy they were. She could almost forgive Rosie's defection. Wasn't love about making the other person happy? That's what her mother had told both her and Kitty when they were seventeen.

Suck it up, Josie. He's just a guy. Another fish in the ocean. A guy with a ponytail. A guy with dark laughing eyes and an engaging smile who just happens to have a rogue dog who just happens to be in love with your *dog.*

Kitty watched as her sister picked up the bakery box by the string and dropped it into the trash compactor.

Damn, her tongue was hanging out for one of the warm, sugary *beignets.*

"How about some coffee, Kitty?"

"No time. I have too much to do in the kitchen. What time do we have to have the food at the Andreponts'?"

"Twelve sharp. Mrs. Andrepont has a wonderful kitchen with lots of room. Everything will go off on schedule. Tonight is going to be tight and close. As soon as I finish my coffee, I'm off to pick up the ladies. I'll be back inside of an hour."

"He seems like a nice guy, Josie. Cut him some slack. Don't let this dog business throw you. I don't want you getting all pissy on me now. Think this through. Hey, the guy gave you the key to his house. He didn't have to do that. You'd kill me if I ever gave Harry a key to this house. Think about *that.*"

Josie turned her back so her sister she wouldn't see the tears that were about to flood her eyes. Why was she crying anyway? That would be the day when she cried over some man. The tears were because of Rosie. God, how she loved that little dog. "Traitor," she muttered.

Five

Paul Brouillette leaned back in his custom-made chair for a better view of the stack of financial reports in front of him. A deep frown etched his brow. He wished he could make the reports disappear. He'd been in the office since six o'clock trying to make that very thing happen. It was eight o'clock now, and his secretary was making coffee. He could smell it, but he knew it wouldn't be half as good as the New Orleans coffee he loved.

He jolted forward and reached for the folder with the red tab; that folder had information about the company his mother managed. It was so far in the red nothing could save it. He'd been subsidizing it for years, and it was like pouring money down an open manhole. The dinner meeting he'd had last night with the accountants had given him a king-size headache that was still with him. The accountant's final words were still ringing in his ears. "Shut it down *now!*" How was he going to do that to his mother? It was all she had left. What about all the cousins and relatives and their families that worked for the company? A severance package meant only months, not years, of security. What would happen to all of them when the severance money ran out? Somehow or other he should have made her listen. Instead, he'd gotten angry when she refused to accept new methods, new advertising, and new packaging. Why wasn't he able to set aside the old hurts? Why did he keep opening up old wounds? Business was business. Family was family. The two couldn't work in harmony for some reason.

The headache continued to hammer at the base of his neck. He needed to work it out. A good long run in Central Park might be the answer. Before he could change his mind, he headed for the lavatory, where he changed into running gear. The phone rang just as he was about to leave the office. He grabbed it on the run and barked into the phone. "Jack! When did you get in? Dinner? Can't make it tonight. You headed for home? Listen, do me a favor. I had to leave Zip with a . . . a friend. She wasn't crazy about taking him. I kind of needled her into it. If you can see your way clear to taking him to my house, I'd appreciate it. I'll call her later and tell her you'll be by to pick him up. Zip knows and likes you. You'll be doing me a hell of a favor, buddy. You'll do it! Great! I owe you, Jack." He listened to the boisterous voice on the other end of the line for a moment. Why was everyone in the world happy but him?

"Get real, Jack. How in the hell do you expect me to turn my back on this thriving family business? I can't do it.

So what if I spent ten years going to school at night to become an architect *after* I got my business degree. It's not something I can work at. We both know that. I know you'll keep offering me a partnership every week, and every week I'll have to tell you the same thing: Family obligations prevent me from accepting your kind, generous offer. So, tell me: What are you building these days? On second thought, don't tell me. I don't want this headache to get worse. What's who like? Oh. She's kind of dumpy—you know, thick around the middle, big feet, hair that stands out like a bush. Pop-bottle glasses. Loves dogs, though. She has a twin in case you're interested. Your loss, buddy. Ah, how long are you planning on staying in N'awlins? That long! Uh-huh. Make sure you treat my dog good. On second thought, I think I'll call my friend and tell her to drop Zip off at the house. I left a key with her. What time are you getting in? I'll time it so he's only alone for a few minutes. He's kind of *skitzy.* Yeah, yeah, that's what I'll do. No sense getting her and the dog worked up. Call me if you think the flight is going to be late. Remember, Zip knows how to open the French doors, so keep a sharp eye. No, I'm not trying to pull a fast one on you. What gave you that idea? You must be between women. You're paranoid. Yeah, yeah. See you in five days."

One last worry off his shoulders. Kind of. Sort of. More or less. Paul smacked his leg in satisfaction. He didn't trust Jack Emery any further than he could throw him. When it came to women, Jack was like a wild stud in a harem. Once he set his eyeballs on Josie Dupré it would be all over but the shouting. He raced by his sputtering secretary. "You'll see me when you see me!"

"What about . . . ? When are you coming . . . ?"

"Deal with it or call André. I'm not taking my beeper, so don't even think about trying to get hold of me. Maybe I'll never come back!"

Paul jabbed at the elevator. "That's the stuff dreams are made of. I'd make a hell of a ski bum. Or a beach bum. On the other hand, I'd make one son of a bitching grade A number one architect," he mumbled as he stepped into the elevator and pressed the button for the lobby.

Paul settled himself comfortably in the cab that would take him to the park, where he would do his ten-mile run. He squeezed his eyes shut. He'd never asked for this damn job. He'd never wanted to run the family business. All he ever wanted was to be an architect. He hated tradition and responsibility. He wished, the way he wished every day of his life, that he had an older brother, even a younger brother. Hell, he'd settle for *anyone* willing to take on his job. His mother had been adamant. *As the only son you will take over from your father.* He'd given up the best years of his life for his family and the business. When was it his turn? When did he get to do what he wanted to do? Never, that's when. Sure he had a good life. Sure he could take days off, weeks, sometimes. But he always had to come back to Cajun spices and cornmeal. He had to stew and fret over the restaurants. He couldn't remember the last time he'd had a peaceful, contented day. Maybe when he was ten or so. No, that's when it all started to fall apart.

"Screw it," he mumbled, tossing the cab driver a twenty-dollar bill. He checked to see that the other twenty was still safe in his pocket. After a ten-mile run he would be in no mood to hike back to his hotel.

He started out slow, building up momentum as he stared straight ahead, his mind refusing to let go of his thoughts. What the hell was wrong with André Hoffauir running Brouillette Enterprises? The guy loved the company, drooled over the Cajun spices and cornmeal, plus he was a natural when it came to the restaurants. He knew every aspect of the business and was family, even if he was a distant cousin. Blood was blood. The problem was Paul's mother. She'd never give the okay to turn the business over to André when she found out Paul was going to close down the cornmeal plant. And yet, André agreed with him.

Three miles into his run, his head was still pounding, and his thoughts were just as jumbled as when he started out. If he'd been more alert, not so focused on his dark thoughts and the path in front of him, he might have seen the thugs coming at him from the left and the right. One moment he was running on the sun-dappled path. A moment later the sunny world around him turned black as he fell to the ground.

"Shit, man! Twenty fucking dollars! You could bench-press that Rolex. Grab it! C'mon, c'mon! We're outta here, man. Go! Go!"

A nanny wheeling a baby in a stroller found Paul Brouillette fifteen minutes later. She dialed 911 on the cell phone the baby's parents insisted she carry with her at all times. She watched, her eyes tearful when the runner's un-conscious body was lifted into the waiting ambulance by EMS workers. In a shaky voice she answered the questions the police asked her over the wailing cries of the child in her care.

Josie looked down at her wrist to check the time. It was hard not to notice the date. Paul had been gone five days, and he hadn't called her. Five days was 120 hours. He said he would call. Men were such bastards. Why did they lie and say they would call when they had no inten-tion of doing so? Jerks. She mentally added Paul's name to her long list of no-call jerks. *Kitty was right: He just wanted a dog-sitter, and I fell for his tired old line. I just might decide to keep this dog.* Possession was nine points of the law.

Her shoulders slumping, Josie checked on the two dogs, who were lying under the oak tree next to the cot-tage. They both looked tired. From the moment she let them out in the morning they ran each other ragged until they both collapsed under the tree. She knew they were only getting their second wind before another game of run and chase. For the moment, they were good for at least an hour. She smiled when they both barked as she made her way to the test kitchen. She noticed Kitty at the window, motioning her to wait outside. She pulled up short and waited.

Her eyes wild, her shoulders shaking, Kitty looked on the verge of tears.

"What's wrong, Kitty?"

"Everything and nothing. I didn't know until today Yvette has cataracts and her vision is almost nil. That's okay because Charlet has a hearing problem and wears *two* hearing aids. She's Yvette's eyes and Yvette is Charlet's ears. It kind of evens out except for the mess they make. Réné can see and hear, but she can't cook worth squat. She does have a plethora of recipes, though. Right now I have her cleaning up. She's been ragging on Yvette and Charlet for two hours. I don't think this is working out, Josie. All they do is fight among themselves. They pretend each dish they're making is for the stars on the soap operas they watch. All morning, when they aren't squabbling, they're whispering about Marie and some family crisis. I tried to . . . you know, listen but they caught on to that real quick. They're sweet and they are adorable but, Josie, this isn't going to work. I don't know how to tell them either."

"I don't think you're going to have to tell them," Josie whispered as she pointed to the three ladies exiting the kitchen, wearing their hats and white gloves. Josie found herself smiling. They looked so genteel, so sweet and charming.

"We are terribly sorry, Miss Dupré, but we won't be able to continue working with you. Marie has just called on the cell phone and we are needed. You will forgive us, no, chère."

"But . . . is something wrong? Can my sister or I help? I'll . . . I'll miss your . . . invaluable help," Kitty managed to croak.

"We feel terrible, deserting you like this but family

must come first. We left our recipes on the counter for you to use. It is the least we can do. Everything is spick-and-span, chère."

"Thank you for all your help, ladies. Are you sure about the recipes?"

"We are sure. Marie said it was the fair thing to do. We always do what she says. We called a cab so as not to trouble you," the sprightly Réné said as she adjusted her floppy-brimmed hat.

"I guess that takes care of that," Josie said. "Call your friend, Kitty. We'll bite the bullet and pay her whatever she wants. It's not like we have a choice. Tell her we'll sign a six-month contract. That will take us through August. We'll be winding down then since you'll be leaving the first of the year. If she's half as good as you are, I might keep her on and keep the business going. Let's just get through this immediate crisis any way we can. Later will take care of itself."

"No word from the big Cajun, huh?"

"I didn't think there would be," Josie said. *Liar, liar, liar.*

"You'll have to hear from him eventually. After all, you have his dog." Kitty twinkled.

"Look, let's not get into any of that because I'm not in the mood. I have to pick up those dishes you ordered. While I'm out, is there anything else you want me to do?"

"You can pick up my dry cleaning. And, you can stop at the music store and pick up that new CD I've been wanting. I just can't seem to find the time to do anything lately. Write this down, Josie, so you get the right CD. It's Corinda Carford. Her CD is called *Mr. Sandman.* Pretty lady with a great voice. There's a song on it that's a hoot. It's called 'The Pantyhose Song.' You're gonna love it. Better yet, pick up two because you aren't getting mine. Listen, I know this is sneaky but why don't you, you know, sort of cruise by Paul's house or hey, go inside and pick up some of Zip's toys. You could, ah . . . look around. You don't have to touch anything. Just look. You do have a key, and he did tell you if you needed anything to go in and get it. You might pick up some clues as to what makes that guy tick. I'd do it!"

"You would, huh? Well, I'm not you! That's right up there with breaking and entering. No, I'm not going to do that. Keep your eye on the dogs, okay?"

"Sure. I think you should go for it. Once in a while you need to do something *unJosie.*"

The moment the Explorer was out of the driveway, Kitty clapped her hands and said to the dogs, "She's gonna do it! I ain't her twin for nothin'."

Zip threw his massive head back and let out an ear-splitting howl. Kitty shivered when Rosie ran under the big dog and cowered.

"Relax. You two aren't going anywhere. I think, Zip, we just inherited you. It's okay, Rosie. He's staying." A smile on her face, Kitty watched as the boxer picked up Rosie by the scruff of the neck and carried her back to the cool moss under the old oak. "Harry loves me like that," Kitty said happily. "He does—he purely does."

* * *

The last of her errands completed, Josie loaded the van and headed for the dry-cleaning shop. She had a good hour before she had to be home to help Kitty load the food into the van for a private dinner. She could stop for coffee, get a double praline crunch ice cream cone or perhaps she could drive by Paul's house. Driving by wasn't the same as going in the way Kitty suggested. "What would you do, Mom? Kitty is so . . . so much like you. Sometimes I wish I was more . . . impulsive like she is. Maybe I'm using the wrong deodorant. He did say he would call. I have his dog. That means he has to come back for him. Do I need more guts? What's wrong with me, Mom? These last few days all I feel like doing is crying. That double praline crunch isn't going to make me feel one bit better. Would you do it, Mom?"

Josie turned the corner but not before she rolled down the window. She eased up on the gas pedal when the overpowering scent of lily of the valley from the house next to Paul's wafted through the window. She blinked and then shivered as she looked around. The flower border on Paul's neighbor's lawn was made up totally of lilies of the valley nestled in and among thickets of spiky monkey grass. Her eyes filled with tears. "I'm taking this as a sign, Mom. I'm gonna do it!"

Her legs felt like jelly as she got out of the car and walked boldly up the driveway to Paul Brouillette's house. He'd said Zip knew how to open the French doors. Maybe it would be better if she walked around the back so the neighbors wouldn't see her and possibly report back to Paul. Maybe the key in her hand would open the French doors. She felt like a thief as she meandered to the back of the house, striving, for a nonchalant pose when she reached the door.

Josie looked over her shoulder. There was nothing to be seen on either side of the house except thick, lush shrubbery pruned to perfection. With a shaking hand she started to fit the key into the lock and then changed her mind. She turned to leave when a light breeze rustled the trees overhead, bringing the scent of lily of the valley to her nostrils. A moment later, the trees were quiet. A dog barked in the distance. A tree frog leaped in front of her. She clapped her hands over her mouth to stifle the squeal that was about to rush past her lips.

There were no squeaks, no groans, no sound at all when the lock turned and the door opened. Josie stepped into an immaculate dining room. In an instant she knew the house was professionally decorated. A bachelor pad done in earth tones. No real color anywhere. She thought it depressing as she walked from room to room. It didn't look like anyone lived in the house. Where were the treasures, the mementos, the family pictures? She eyed the expensive silk plants with a jaundiced eye. She hated silk plants. She decided she also hated the faceless decorator who had taken such modern liberties with the beautiful old house.

Josie peeked into the kitchen. Kitty would love the sterile, stainless-steel area. She wouldn't like the wrought-iron table and chairs, though. There was no centerpiece on the table, no colorful place mats or napkins, no cushions on the hard, iron chairs. She shuddered. How could Paul Brouillette live in such a cold, impersonal house? Maybe he didn't really live here; maybe he just came back and forth. Tentatively she opened the huge refrigerator. Her jaw dropped at the shelves full of food.

Where were Zip's things, his bed, his toys? Maybe Zip was just a dog to Paul. A dog he fed and walked. She felt a frown building between her eyebrows. A dog was a commitment, a responsibility, a member of the family.

The frown stayed with Josie as she made her way to the second floor. She told herself going to the second floor was simply to look for Zip's things. Certainly not to check out Paul's bedroom. She'd never do something like that. Kitty would, but she wouldn't. Kitty would want to know if he wore boxers or jockeys.

The doors to three of the bedrooms stood open. Josie peeked into each room. Clean, neat, professionally decorated like the downstairs. The bathrooms were done in pastel shades with matching towels and rugs. Even the soap matched. Josie winced. Were these rooms ever used? Did Paul entertain or have guests? She wondered if there was anything feminine in his room or bathroom. Someone who stayed over and left things behind.

Josie had to coax herself to open the door to what she assumed was Paul's bedroom. Three times her hand reached out to turn the knob and three times she pulled it back. Checking out the rest of the house was one thing, but if she went into this room, she was invading Paul's privacy.

On the fourth try she allowed her hand to close over

the knob. She turned it slowly, sucking in her breath as she did so. It was dim and cool inside and she had to squint to see the dim shapes of the furniture. She had the impression of a large, square room with equally large furniture. She squeezed her eyes shut and then reopened them in hopes of a better look. Here there were photographs, four in all on top of the long dresser. As her eyes adjusted to the dimness in the room she allowed her gaze to sweep past the open bathroom door, the pile of clothes outside the door, to the night tables and the long king-size bed, where someone was sleeping.

Josie thought her blood froze in her veins in that one second. *Someone sleeping.* She clapped her hand over her mouth to keep from calling out. *You bastard! You smart-ass bastard. You're here sleeping while I stew and fret about why you didn't call me. Kitty was right. All you wanted was someone to watch your dog.*

Josie backed away from the open doorway and reached out to close it quietly. She wasn't aware that she was crying until she was outside. Inside the Explorer, she reached for a tissue and blew her nose. The scent of lily of the valley was so strong she got back out of the car and walked across the lawn to Paul's neighbor's house, where she dropped to her knees to sniff the tiny flowers. There was hardly any scent at all. She moved along on her knees, realizing how stupid she must look to anyone watching. She didn't care. Satisfied, she stood up and walked back to the Explorer. She felt light-headed when she leaned back in the driver's seat to let the light flower scent wash over her. "Oh, Mom," she wailed.

* * *

He knew he was in a hospital. He could tell by the smell and the way everyone was whispering. He knew a thing or two about hospitals. People died in hospitals. His father had died in one, his three stepfathers had died in hospitals and so had his two sisters. He knew he had to open his eyes, but the moment he did that, the voices in the room would start to talk to him, ask him questions. He didn't want to talk, and he certainly didn't want to answer questions. He needed to think. He needed to remember how he got here. He knew he would never voluntarily go to a hospital on his own. That had to mean he had had an accident of some kind, and someone else brought him here. He wanted to move his legs and arms, test his fingers, open his eyes but if he did that the voices would know he was awake. Better to wait and think. He heard the words *John Doe Number 4*. Were they referring to him? Was he a John Doe? It must mean they didn't know his name. He remembered then. He'd been running in the park. All he had on him was a twenty-dollar bill for the taxi ride after his run. Did he trip and fall? Was he mugged? How had he gotten here? Well, the only way he was going to find out was to open his eyes and ask questions. He did just that.

There were five people in the room: two doctors and three nurses. "What happened to me? How long have I been here?" he whispered.

Instead of answering his questions, the tall distinguished doctor asked one of his own: "How many fingers am I holding up?"

"Three. What's wrong with me?"

"Are you in any pain?" the doctor asked, ignoring that question, too.

"My head and neck hurt. I had a headache when I started out. What the hell happened to me?"

"We don't know. We're assuming you were mugged. You had no ID on you when you were brought in. You had no watch, no rings, no money. It was a logical conclusion. A nanny walking a baby in the park called 911 and you were brought here by ambulance. You have a severe concussion. Your name please."

"Paul Brouillette. How long have I been here?"

"This is your fifth day. You were unconscious for nearly twenty-four hours. For the last few days you've been slipping in and out. We tried to talk to you, but you kept falling asleep. Your vital signs are good. That nasty headache is going to stay with you for a few more days. What you need now is rest and some solid food. You should be able to leave here in a day or so. Now, we need to take down your insurance information. Someone from the business office will be up in a little while to do that. For now we want to draw some blood, run some tests, and take your blood pressure. By the way, I'm Dr. Slobodian and this is Dr. Entwhistle. These lovely nurses are Karen, Janet, and Andrea. I'll check back on you when I make rounds this evening. Sleep and relax, Mr. Brouillette. It's the best thing for you."

"I need to make some telephone calls," Paul said wearily.

"The nurses will make them for you."

He thought nurses wore little starched caps and rustled when they walked. These women moved soundlessly and wore squashed-up blue paper hats and blue paper booties. On television they only wore getups like that in the operating room.

"Now, Mr. Brouillette, who would you like me to call?" one of the nurses asked cheerfully.

Jack Emery? The office? His mother? Josie Dupré? Zip? "I can't remember," he lied. He sniffed. "Did someone send me flowers?"

"I don't think so, Mr. Brouillette. Why do you ask?"

"I guess it's your perfume I smell."

The nurse laughed. "We aren't allowed to wear perfume. I don't smell anything. Are you sure it isn't the hospital smell?"

"Those little white flowers that look like tiny bells," Paul said, sniffing again.

"You must mean lilies of the valley. I have some in my flower garden. They smell wonderful. I'm sorry to disappoint you, sir. Sometimes a concussion strengthens the senses or possibly someone wearing perfume walked down the hall. That must be it. A visitor wearing perfume. Now, aren't you glad we solved that little mystery? This isn't going to hurt," the nurse said as she strapped on the blood-pressure cuff to his upper arm. Paul was asleep before she nodded in satisfaction and proceeded to jot down the numbers on the chart at the end of his bed.

Jack Emery padded barefoot down the long flight of stairs and out to the kitchen, where he searched for coffee.

When he saw the pot was empty and he would have to make his own, he groaned. While the coffee dripped he swigged down half a quart of ice-cold tomato juice, swearing he was never going to tie one on again. He'd had his share of hangovers during what he called his hellion years, but this one was the queen mother of hangovers. Damn! Those last two drinks were what had done him in. Since he couldn't see his car in the driveway, that had to mean he had the good sense to take a taxi, or else one of his friends had dumped him off. What the hell had he been celebrating anyway? John Connors's big promotion? Like he really cared if John Connors got promoted or not. It was just an excuse on his end to party a little too hearty. Well, that would be it for another six months.

Jack rubbed his temples. Today was going to be a recovery day. Thank God he owned his own company and didn't have to report to some tight-assed, surly boss. Besides, there was something he was supposed to do today. What the hell was it? Yeah, yeah, he was supposed to pick up Zip. Where the hell was the piece of paper with the name and address? Pants pocket, jacket pocket? That meant he had to go upstairs to get it. Call ahead. It was always good to call ahead and set things up. That's what he would do the minute he made his way upstairs. He finished off the tomato juice and a second cup of coffee. He didn't feel one bit better. He started to feel worse when he looked at the clock and knew he wouldn't be able to make his luncheon date with Marissa Gaffney no matter how hard he tried. *Call now and get it over with.*

His head pounding, he padded over to the phone and

dialed the number from memory. "It's Jack, Marissa. I'm sorry but I have to cancel lunch. The truth is, I'm dog-sitting. I have one hell of a hangover, and I don't have a car at the moment. I'm staying at Paul's house to watch Zip. I owed him a couple of favors. Listen, how about dinner to-morrow night instead? I'm sorry about lunch. Is dinner on or off? Call me."

Jack groaned. *Oh well, there are other fish in the sea. But not like Marissa.* He knew he had some major sucking up to do, and he would do it because he didn't want to lose her. Marissa was *okay.*

An hour later, his hair still damp from the shower, Jack got dressed in khaki shorts and a Polo T-shirt and open-toed sandals. He searched his trouser pockets as well as his jacket pockets for the address and phone number of Zip's temporary guardian. There was no paper to be found. Somehow he must have lost it. Shit! Now what was he supposed to do? Paul would be fit to be tied.

Jack perched on the side of the bed, his head pounding as he dialed Paul's private New York number. He cursed when he got his voice-mail. "Hey, good buddy, I hate to admit this but I lost Zip's info. Can you call me here at the house and give me the number of the fat chick with the big feet? I'll go right over there and pick him up. I'll wait for your call. It's eleven-thirty now."

At four-thirty, his headache still with him, Jack called the main number of Brouillette Enterprises and asked for Paul. "You must have some idea of where he is. Fine, fine, tell him to call me as soon as he gets back. I'll wait for his call."

At six o'clock, tired of sitting around, Jack walked into the family room, which now belonged to Zip. Outside of FAO Schwarz, he'd never seen such an array of toys, beds, collars, leashes, and even a red wagon. Zip's room. Paul had a chair and a small television set. The rest of the room was totally Zip's. He looked at the shelf over the wet bar. Every dog treat known to an animal lover was on the shelf. He reached for one of the hearty-looking leashes and made the decision to canvass the neighborhood. Paul had said it was within walking distance. He could call out to the dog, whistle, do whatever it took. The poor thing was probably sitting by the door whining and crying to go home. What kind of fun would he have with a fat chick with big feet? Zip was a man's dog. A real man's dog.

"I'm coming, buddy. I'm coming."

Six

"Okay, that's the last of it," Kitty said, blowing a wisp of hair off her cheek. "I think the Soileaus are going to be delighted with this intimate little dinner party for two. Celia reminds me of you—she can't cook worth a darn. Her husband loves her anyway. You should see the diamond choker he's giving his little cupcake. It's got to be at least five carats. And she doesn't do housework either. She has a housekeeper, and a nanny for her little guy. We must be doing something wrong."

"Everything will go wonderfully. I just wonder what the little cupcake is going to do when and if we go out of business. We've been serving their dinners every weekend for three years," Josie grumbled. Some people just seemed to step in good luck. Unlike her, who couldn't seem to do anything right where men were concerned.

"They'll hire another caterer who won't be half as good. You look anxious, Josie. Is something wrong?"

"No. I've had this weird feeling all day. I can't put my

finger on it. He's back, you know. Back and he didn't call. We still have his dog, too."

"What's with that *we* stuff?" Kitty said, slamming the door of the van. "*You* still have his dog. Maybe he got in late; maybe the phones don't work. Maybe he's sick. Maybe he's in love with you and too shy to make another overture. Maybe a lot of things. Time will tell the tale."

"I hate leaving the dogs."

"Get off it, Josie. You just want to stay home in case the phone rings. That's why we have three different answering machines. It will be a good thing if he does call and you aren't here."

"I'm not playing anything. You know what? I'm *pissed.*"

"Oooh, Josie, Mom would wash your mouth out with soap. N'awlins ladies do not use such language. Ever."

"They don't run *naked* through the rain slurping on a mango either," Josie snapped.

"Touché, big sister. C'mon, let's get this show on the road."

"What is it we're serving again? For some reason I can't seem to remember anything these past few days."

"You asked me that six times today. For the seventh time, we are serving baked oysters with braised leeks and tasso Hollandaise. Since this is a special night for our clients, I chose oysters because they have a reputation as an aphrodisiac. Now, how many times have you seen a car sticker that read: Eat Louisiana oysters and live longer? Thousands, right? See, perfect choice. We also have roasted eggplant and garlic soup. We have a side dish of creole-spiced blue crab with green onion dipping sauce. Celia passed on a salad this time and wanted us to double up on the dessert. I made fresh coconut ice cream and *profiteroles*. I made enough so they can eat this stuff all week. As usual, it will tide them over until next weekend. How's it sound?"

"Wonderful. They'll go to bed drunk on good food."

"And we laugh all the way to the bank. Lighten up, Josie. You look way too grim."

Josie bared her teeth in a grimace. "Is that better?"

Kitty sighed. "No, but I guess it will have to do."

Jack Emery loped down the street, calling Zip's name and whistling. He was three houses away from Dupré Catering when a boy of eight or so stopped, his bike squealing on the sidewalk.

"You lose your dog, mister? For five bucks I can help you find him. What's he look like?"

"Big boxer with ears standing straight up. Brown and white. Big dog. I didn't lose him, but I did lose the paper with the woman's name on it who's watching him. His name is Zip."

"I seen him. Yeah, I did, mister. I seen her pulling him in a wagon. Nah, that's wrong, some guy was pulling him and the lady was pulling the little dog in a wagon. I'm telling you, I seen him, mister."

"Give me an address and the five bucks is yours, and you don't even have to go looking for him."

"Right there where that sign is in the driveway. Miss Josie is the lady. Miss Kitty, she don't have no truck with dogs. She cooks."

Jack wondered if he was being had as he forked over a five dollar bill.

"Go around to the back, mister. Them dogs are always fenced in. That's so they can't get out. The one with the big ears could jump the fence, but he don't. He likes it there. See ya, mister."

Jack walked up the driveway, his eyes and ears alert. He tucked his tongue down and pursed his lips. A shrill whistle ripped through the air. He was rewarded with a howl that made his short-cropped sandy hair stand on end. "Yo, boy. It's me, Jack! Where are you, Zip?"

A second earsplitting howl rocked the quiet evening. Jack followed the sound. He heard the door rattle on the back porch as he climbed the steps. He rang the bell and waited. "Anyone home?" Jack bellowed. He jabbed at the bell again and again. "Guess the fat lady with the big feet left you all alone. Paul isn't going to like that one little bit." He jiggled the handle but it held tight. "I'll just sit right here and wait for your . . . the lady to get home. I missed you, big guy. Man, do I have some stories to tell you."

He heard the noise, felt the vibration, and then he was tumbling down the steps to the lawn. "What the hell . . . ? Zip! How the hell? Oh, oh, you pushed open the door. That lady isn't going to like that. No, siree. And what's this?" he said, reaching for Rosie, who whined as he held her up to his cheek. She was soft and cuddly, kind of like Marissa when she was in one of her cuddly moods. A heartbeat later, he was astounded when Zip reached up and daintily removed Rosie from his grasp. He sat her down right between his two big front paws.

"I get it—it's a package deal. You and her. I know she's a girl. Paul didn't say he got a new dog. Or, does this little beauty belong here? Probably. That's going to be a problem. The door's broken, so we can't leave her here. That means she has to come with us. Okay, we'll take her with us, and I'll bring her back in the morning." Zip reared backward, his right front paw pulling Rosie with him. "I guess I said the wrong thing. Okay, we won't bring her back. We'll take it on the lam and let Paul deal with the chick with the big feet. I wonder what they do to dog-nappers. Paul can worry about that, too. We'll say she followed us. Yeah, yeah, that's what we'll say. But let's see how this grabs you. We're switching up here and going to *my* house instead of Paul's house. I don't feel like dealing with any women right now, and that includes Marissa. We're all happy campers now, right?"

"Woof."

"Woof."

"Celia's husband did us proud tonight, Kitty. A hundred dollar tip! What *does* that guy do for a living? Boy, did you see them eat? I bet he'd hire you to cook for him every day if he could. I don't think you made enough food to last all week, though."

"They'll order something in or go the fast-food route. Then they'll drool for our stuff for two days. Next week Celia said her husband wants potato-crusted lobster tails on a bed of mugbug mashed potatoes, sweet water prawns over spinach *pappardelle* with a champagne and salmon roe butter sauce, poke salad with sesame vinaigrette. For dessert, *malassadas* with extra pastry cream, macaroon tartlets with some creole cream cheese ice cream. I thought I would throw in a praline cream pie just for the heck of it. Oh, I almost forgot. He said he would look on us real favorably if I could somehow manage to whip up a favorite of his—duck Andouille, and scallion pancakes with ginger orange sauce. Of course I said okay. I can make them while I'm there so they'll be hot when we serve them."

"The man will die if he eats all that," Josie sputtered. "Celia will get fat!"

"No doubt. You asked me what he does for a living. He's a venture capitalist. I don't even know what that is, but he makes tons of money."

"I'm tired just thinking about all that food. Let's do the dishes in the morning. I just want to take a shower and go to bed. Did they pay for the wine tonight?"

"Yep, all four bottles. Everything was included in the one check. I'll lock the car and be in in a minute. I don't hear the dogs barking."

"They're probably sound asleep and snoring. For a little dog, Rosie snores real loud. Kittyyyyy!"

"What? What's wrong?"

"Look! The door is broken—it's off the hinges. Zip

got out. Oh, God, what am I going to tell Paul? Rosie! Come here, Rosie. Where are you, baby? Help me look for her, Kitty. Oh, God, what if she went on the run with Zip. People steal dogs all the time for experiments."

"Didn't you lock the door Josie?"

"Of course I locked the door. One swipe of his paw and Zip can move the dead bolt. You saw him do it. He got the big door open and just slammed through the screen door. Maybe Paul came here and he wanted out. That's it. I bet he's at Paul's house. Keep looking, Kitty, while I call. There's no answer," she said, disgust ringing in her voice. "I'm going over there!"

"Not without me, you aren't. I'll drive."

"That son of a bitch stole my dog. I know it. How could he do that, Kitty?"

"We don't know that he did, Josie. If he did, I'll help you kill him. I told you not to take his dog. Did you listen? No, you did not."

Josie was out of the car before Kitty turned off the engine. She raced around the back of the house to the French doors. A second later she was inside, her hand on the light switch. "Rosie! Rosie! Come on, baby. Damn, they aren't here! Zip would be barreling through the house barking his head off. Unless they're upstairs in his room and the door is closed." She galloped up the steps, taking them two at a time as she called her dog's name over and over, Kitty just behind her.

"There's no one here, Kitty. The bed is unmade. There was no car in the driveway."

"Maybe he's out walking them," Kitty said. "It is a possibility."

"No, it isn't, and you know it. He's gone. The dogs are gone. The house is dark. He took my dog!"

"Hey, look at these pictures. They look familiar. Do they look familiar to you, Josie?"

Josie barely glanced in the direction of the long dresser. "No, and I'm not interested in his family. Who cares what they look like? I want my dog!"

"Are you sure he was here today?"

"I saw him with my own eyes. He was sleeping in that damn bed! That bed!" Josie said, pointing to the king-size bed. He's probably out wining and dining some other fool so she'll watch his dog and mine, too. Do you have any idea how much I hate that man? Well, do you?"

"I think I have a pretty good idea. Let's drive around with the windows down. We can call out."

"It's almost midnight. Do you want to get locked up for disturbing the peace?" Josie said. "What if they ran off somewhere? Rosie doesn't know how to fend for herself."

"Get in the car, Josie. We'll drive around real slow. If they're on the loose, they'll pick up our scent. For now it's all we can do. In the morning you can call his offices or come back to the house. We'll think of something by then. Hey, maybe they'll be on the porch waiting for us when we get home."

It was two o'clock when Kitty turned off the headlights of the Explorer. There were no joyful barks coming from the back porch. She felt like crying. "I'll make some coffee, and you can call the police. The night patrols might spot them if they are on the loose. I know they're safe, Josie. I just know it."

Josie nodded, her face miserable.

"And how are we feeling this morning, Mr. Brouillette?" a young nurse asked cheerfully.

"*We* aren't feeling much better than *we* felt last night," Paul muttered. "Let's just skip the sponge bath."

"Now, Mr. Brouillette, you know we can't do that. Rules are rules. Germs are germs. How's the headache?"

"I still have it. What are the chances of me going home today?"

"About the same as me going to Hawaii when I get off duty. We'll ask the doctor when he makes rounds. In case you forgot, you have a severe concussion, Mr. Brouillette. Do you need someone to make phone calls for you? If you hire a private duty nurse, the doctor might consider discharging you a little early. It's something to think about."

Paul suffered through the sponge bath, his teeth clenched in frustration.

"This is just an off-the-wall question, Mr. Brouillette, but do you know how to relax?"

"Of course I know how to relax. Why do you ask?"

"Because you're much too tense. The headache might ease up if you'd loosen up."

Paul closed his eyes. She was probably right. As Jack would say, he was wired to the nth degree. And why shouldn't he be wired? He'd been mugged and left to die in the park. He made a mental note to ask for the name of the nanny so he could call and thank her for her intervention. He'd have his secretary send her a nice gift of appreciation.

He thought about Josie Dupré and the dogs. A tiny smile tugged at the corners of his mouth. She was nice. Pretty even, with that wild bush of hair. The smile got wider when he thought of the baseball cap he'd bought her and how pleased she'd been. He remembered her reaction when he dumped her in the rain puddle. What was she doing right now? Was she sitting in her pretty breakfast nook with the dogs at her feet drinking her early-morning coffee? He wished he could sprout wings and fly out of the room.

Paul's eyes started to burn. He knuckled them. When he opened them, he noticed a beautiful woman in a pink dress glance into his room. He sniffed when the faint scent of lily of the valley wafted into the room. The same visitor from yesterday. He closed his eyes. When he opened them again, he was back in the courtyard in the French Quarter. He was ten years old and he was crying because he didn't understand what was happening to his family. Everyone was crying. He could see them through the doorway. All he knew was what the housekeeper told him and what he had seen with his own eyes. The white truck with the flashing lights had taken his sixteen-year-old sister away and she was never coming back. Just the way Jackie never came back. He'd run to his mother shouting, "*Mère, Mère, what's wrong?*" His mother had pushed him away and he fell. She didn't care because she was crying so hard her shoulders were shaking. She never stopped crying. She never looked at him again either. She looked over his head, at his feet, or to the side of him. At night he waited for her to come to his room to kiss him good night or to tell him a little story about what happened during the day. She never came again. Never. Old Réné came, though, waddling down the hall in her slippered feet. She'd hug him, smooth back his hair, listen to his prayers, and ask him if he had brushed his teeth. And always, the last thing she'd say before she turned off the light was, "Someday when you are older, you'll understand." Someday was a long time coming and when it had come, he no longer cared that his mother didn't love him and didn't want anything to do with him.

His name was Bushy and he was a little dog Réné smuggled into the house for him. It was their secret. God, how he loved that little dog. After Bushy there was Quincy and then Basil and Corky. All loved and adored.

Paul's eyes snapped open when the scent of lily of the valley wafted into his room again. He stared at the open doorway and saw a pale swish of pink. He wished he was the patient the woman was visiting. He wondered who she was and if someone she loved was seriously ill. He hoped not.

Paul rang the bell attached to the rail on the side of his bed. A candy striper came on the run. "I need someone to make a phone call for me."

"I'll be glad to do it for you, sir," the young girl smiled.

"Get a piece of paper so you can write this down. I want you to say exactly what I tell you. Can you do that?"

"Absolutely, sir. I'll be back in a minute."

The candy striper, who said her name was Jennifer, sat down primly, a pad and pencil poised on her lap. "I'm ready, sir."

"You're calling André Hoffauir at Brouillette Enterprises. I'll give you the number when we're finished. Tell him Paul asked you to call. Something came up, and I won't be back in the office for some time. Tell him he's totally in charge and to do whatever he sees fit. Tell him he answers to no one but me, not even my mother. Is that clear?"

"Yes, sir, very clear."

"Do not tell André I'm in the hospital. If he asks, tell him you don't know where I am or where I'm going. Just say you're delivering a message and that I will be in touch at some point."

"Very good, sir. I can do this. Do you want me to report back and tell you what he said?"

"Yes. Can you do it now?"

"Right away, sir."

The pink dress swished by again and so did the light flowery scent. Paul blinked and then rubbed his eyes with his knuckles when the pretty woman smiled and offered a lazy wink. Double vision, imaginary vision, mirages, flower-scented people. Paul closed his eyes and then opened them immediately. He didn't want the candy striper to think he was sleeping.

"Sir, I delivered your message. Mr. Hoffauir said I should tell you, if I spoke to you again, to have a hell of a good time. He said he'll man the ship just the way you did and not to worry about a thing. He said he will also handle the business with Marie. He said you would know what that meant. He said he will make you proud of him, and you are not to worry about a thing. He really didn't ask any questions about you, so I didn't have to fib."

"Thank you very much, Jennifer. Do you know who the lady is in the pink dress? She keeps going past this room. She's pretty, and she wears nice perfume."

Jennifer frowned. "Do you mean a visitor or maybe a volunteer?"

"I don't know. She was here yesterday, too. I remember the perfume."

"It's too early for visitors. All the volunteers wear blue smocks. There are only two patients at the end of this hall, Mr. O'Brien and Mr. Stevens. Their wives come at night because they work during the day. As far as I know neither one has had other visitors. Both Mr. O'Brien and Mr. Stevens have been in the physical-therapy room since breakfast. I guess that doesn't help you much, does it?"

"Maybe I was dreaming or half-asleep or something," Paul mumbled. "Then again, maybe it's my concussion. Thank you. I appreciate you making the call for me. Later on, I need you to make a few more once I get my thoughts straight. Can you come back?"

"Just press the call button on the rail, and I'll be back. It's a light day. Most of the patients are leaving this morning."

Two hours later, Paul woke slowly. He stretched his legs and groaned. He was stiff and sore, but his pounding headache was almost gone. He heaved a sigh of relief. He tried a smile when the young candy striper poked her head in the door. "You're awake, Mr. Brouillette. Do you want me to make those calls for you now? I have my pad and pencil. I'm also supposed to tell you lunch will be here in fifteen minutes." She wrinkled her nose to show what she thought of the lunch that was about to be served.

"I'm ready. The first call is to Miss Josie Dupré. The second is to Paul Emery. Tell Miss Dupré that I've been unavoidably detained. Tell her I'll make it up to her. Don't give any details. When you call Mr. Emery, just tell him I'm counting on him to take care of Zip and to guard him with his life. Tell him, too, that I'll be in touch in a few days. This is Miss Dupré's phone number . . ."

"Okay, I got it all. I'll bring your lunch on my way back. By the way, the charge nurse said no one wearing a pink dress has been on the floor this morning. She really has an eagle eye, so she would know."

"I guess I was dreaming."

"Guess so," the candy striper said, tripping out of the room. "Is there anything else I can get you?"

"A bottle of scotch."

The young girl giggled. "You know I can't do that, Mr. Brouillette."

Paul sighed. God, how he hated hospitals. He hated the smells, the canvas curtains that surrounded his bed, and he hated the sounds coming from the hallway. He wished he could swing his legs over the side of the bed and leave. Hell, he didn't even know where his clothes were, and he wasn't about to go traipsing around in the nightgown he was wearing with his ass hanging out. He wondered if he was being punished for sins he'd committed in his life.

Paul closed his eyes and thought about Josie Dupré. He wondered what she would say when he told her he wanted to hire her for a special Mother's Day event, if only he could find his sister's husband and child. What better gift to give his mother? The grandchild she hadn't seen in years and years. The daughter of her own daughter. He made a mental note to call the detective agency to inquire as to progress. In six months he should have found something. There had been so many hot leads that turned cold in the beginning. Now it was just tiresome gumshoe work, as the detective put it. His parting shot had been that if you persevered you would prevail.

Jack looked at the phone in his hand, the dial tone ringing in his ear. A deep frown spread across his brow. What the hell was Paul up to now? More to the point, where the hell was he? "I bet you planned this all along, you *schmuck,*" he mumbled. Zip whined at his feet. With Paul a few more days could well turn into three months. He should know. He'd fallen for Paul's tricks before. In the end, what was a few more days? He loved Zip, and the little hairball was starting to grow on him. He tried not to think of the owner with the big feet and what she was going through. Maybe he should take both dogs back and suffer the consequences. Yeah, that's what he would do as soon as he showered and shaved. He tried not to make eye contact with either dog because he was convinced they could read his mind. Better to plop them in his car, which was returned during the night, and drive over to the house where he picked up the dogs.

Paul finished his coffee and then poured another cup, which he took with him to the upstairs shower. He was ready to go in less than an hour. He spent another five minutes trying to look contrite in front of the mirror. Satisfied, he called the dogs. "Got some errands to run, Zip. Want to come along?"

The big boxer raced to the door, Rosie on his heels. Getting them in the car was going to be the true test. In the end he had no trouble when he picked up Rosie and settled her on the backseat. He lost his balance and went flying into a flower bed when Zip raced past him and leaped onto the backseat.

"You need some manners, Zip my boy," Jack grumbled as he started up the car. Ten minutes later he barely missed hitting a telephone pole when Zip howled in his ear. "Yeah, this is the place. I'm going to have to pay for that door you played with last night. Hold it, hold it! Let me turn the damn car off first."

Whoever she was, she was mad as hell. He watched to see if smoke would billow out of her ears before he opened the car door.

"You stole my dogs, you son of a bitch! I see them in your car. Open the door before I pop you good." Not bothering to wait for her order to be obeyed, Josie yanked at the door. Both dogs hit the driveway running. "Get back here, Rosie! Who are you? I'm calling the police! You stand right there, mister, and don't even think about moving."

"Hey . . . listen . . . You got this all wrong . . . I . . ."

"Shut up!"

"Don't tell me to shut up! I'm doing you a favor. I brought your dog back. I didn't know it was a package deal. You should thank me. Where's the lady with the . . . ?"

"With the what?"

"The fat one with the big feet. Where is she? Wild-looking hair! Paul said she was watching Zip. He went through the door when I came to get him. Obviously, you weren't home. I couldn't leave the little one, so I took her, too. I called you several times. You don't answer your phone either."

Josie tried to digest the information. Fat lady, big feet, wild hair! He came to get Zip. "Did Paul send you here?" Josie snarled.

"Yes, ma'am, he did. Now if you'll just fetch the other lady, I'll explain and take Zip with me. I'll be happy to pay for the screen door."

"This is the second screen door Mr. Brouillette has ruined for me. Damn straight you'll pay for it. There is no fat lady here with big feet. It's just me and my sister. I don't appreciate your humor, and I sure as hell don't appreciate Mr. Brouillette's humor either. Where is he?"

"He . . . ah . . . he said he was delayed. I haven't talked to him in a few days. I did get a message this morning. He said he was going to call you. That's Paul for you," Jack said, throwing his hands in the air. She was nice. Too nice for Paul. Hell, she looked even better than Marissa. He turned on the charm. "I really am sorry about all this. I thought I was doing a friend a favor. Somehow Paul just—what he does is . . . hell, he's a nice guy, but you know, not dependable at all. Think about it. You had his dog. I took his dog. I brought them back. You're angry. I'm angry. And where is Paul? Do we know? No, we do not know. He leaves messages. Nice guy, though. Real nice guy. You aren't fat at all, and your feet look pretty good to me. I like your hair. I love wild hair. I mean, I really like wild hair. When a woman has wild hair there's so much to hang on to. Listen, how would you like to have dinner with me?"

"Not in this lifetime. Do you have any idea how worried I've been? I drove around all night looking for those dogs. I called the police, sat by the phone. This is unacceptable."

"I am so sorry, and you are right—it is unacceptable. However, you can't shoot the messenger because you don't like the message. We need to lay the blame where it belongs: on Paul," Jack said virtuously. "Why don't we have dinner this evening and talk this over? In the meantime I can call the hardware store and have someone come to fix your screen door." At Josie's undecided look he switched gears. "Hey, I'm a nice guy. I clean up good. I have manners, and my teeth are my own. Look at this hair—it's not receding one little bit. I own my own business, and I know how to be charming. You can bring your sister if you want. I love animals. I really do. That's why Paul trusts me with his."

A devil perched itself on Josie's shoulder. "Sure, why not? What time?"

"How does eight sound?" Jack said gleefully as he smacked his hands together.

"Eight sounds good. Now, about Zip. He won't go without Rosie, so that means he has to stay here. I'll keep them for now. Do you have any idea when Paul will be back?"

"I didn't speak to him. Someone called and left a message. You know what I know. You and Paul . . . are you . . . ? What I mean is, are you two, you know, an item?"

Josie laughed, a bitter angry sound. "Hardly."

"By the way, I'm Jack Emery." *You screwed this one up, Paul. You snooze, you lose.*

"Josie Dupré," Josie said, holding out her hand. She got goose bumps when Jack brought her hand to his lips. She laughed when she saw the merriment in his eyes. It might be a fun evening. Anything was better than sitting home with two dogs mooning over each other.

"I'll see you tonight then. I'm punctual."

"Good. So am I.

Josie watched until the BMW was out of sight.

Life was just one surprise after another.

Seven

He was just as tall as Paul, just as slim. Where Paul was dark, Jack was fair. Same weight. Same size. Both had a sense of humor, but where Paul's was dry and droll, Jack was ebullient, and he literally danced when he got off a zinger, his eyes sparkling with glee.

"This is just a hole-in-the-wall restaurant, but they serve the best, and I do mean the best, shrimp *boulettes* and corn puppies. That's the menu. Fried corn on the cob is the side dish. No rolls, no salad. Dark beer. I come here at least once a week. It's dark, it's dingy, and probably a little on the dirty side, but you can't beat the food. If you don't like it, we can go someplace else," Jack said, holding the door for Josie.

Josie stepped gingerly over the threshold. It was everything Jack said it was, maybe a little dirtier. Kitty would throw up her hands in horror. She just knew there would be paper plates and hard plastic glasses for the beer and paper napkins.

He was laughing at her, enjoying her discomfort. "Guess you've never been to a place like this, huh?"

"When I was in college, I went to a few places like this. Standing room only and the food was wonderful. I'm taking you at your word." He was good-looking, with an infectious smile. It was hard not to respond to his light-heartedness. Before she knew it, she was giggling and laughing and having the time of her life.

"So the dogs are safe?"

"My sister is watching them. I can't explain the attraction the two of them have for each other. Zip is a really good dog. I don't know what's going to happen when Paul finally takes him home. Rosie will have a broken heart."

"Speaking of Paul, did you get a message?"

"Yes," Josie said curtly.

"Is Paul Brouillette something we shouldn't be talking about? I see something in your face and in your eyes that tells me this is a no-win zone."

"What might that be?" Josie asked lightly.

"That your heart belongs to the big Cajun. Hey, that's okay. Paul is a great guy. We've been friends forever. I think your ego was a bit bruised when I came by and asked you to dinner, and that's why you accepted. That's okay, too. I'm more or less involved with someone right now. Let's just have a good time and then head over to Bourbon Street. I want to take you to Port Orleans to hear Butterfunck. I could listen to those guys all night long. Anytime I have visitors, that's the first place I take them."

Josie smiled. "Johnny Pappas, guitar and lead vocals, Réné Richard on bass, and Trey Crain on drums, right? How can you forget a name like Butterfunck?"

Jack's eyebrows shot upward. "How'd you know?"

"My sister Kitty goes to listen to them all the time. They're friends. I bet you didn't know Johnny is marrying Jeanne. He is. She's cute as a button. I asked Paul to take me one night. You're right—they're great. We went to Preservation Hall that night, too. It poured rain the whole time."

An hour later Josie leaned back in her chair. "You were right. That's some of the best food I've ever eaten. I'll have to come here again. Do you have *any* idea when Paul will be back?"

"No, I'm sorry, I don't. Paul never does anything without a reason, so whatever it is that's keeping him away, it must be important. He's a kind, considerate guy. You're hung up on him, aren't you?"

"Now where did you get an idea like that?" Josie mumbled.

"From you. It's written all over your face. Do you want to talk about it?"

"No. Yes. Maybe. No. No, I don't."

"Then why don't I pay the bill so we can get out of here?"

"He's here. I saw him sleeping in his bed. I went over to the house to look for some of Zip's things, and there he was, sound asleep, while I was taking care of his dog. He didn't call the way he said he would. I let it get out of hand. He just wanted someone to take care of his dog, and I'm a real sucker when it comes to animals."

Jack fished in his wallet for his credit card. "When was this?"

"Yesterday."

"That was me! I slept at Paul's house. It's a long story. I partied a little too hearty and had to leave my car behind. It was one of those going-away parties with lots of guys and good wishes, that kind of thing. I'm telling you, it was *me.*"

The relief on Josie's face was so apparent, Jack burst out laughing. "Yep, that really tells me you're not hung up on the guy. Okay, we're outta here. Butterfunck, here we come." Josie linked her arm with Jack's. *Now* she could enjoy the evening.

Paul Brouillette shook the doctor's hand before he accepted a short list of instructions.

"Just take it a little easy for a few weeks. No mountain climbing, no jogging or running. No lifting. Everything else in moderation. I'd like you to check back with me in a month for a follow-up. Make the appointment when you leave. We'll call the day before as a reminder."

Paul nodded. Earlier the doctor had said he was golden, which meant he was okay. "You're good to go, Mr. Brouillette." The words were music to his ears. Now he could dismiss the tyrant who oversaw his ten-day recovery. He could go back to the office if he wanted to or he could hop on a plane and head for New Orleans. He could take long walks with Zip, take Josie Dupré out to dinner. A frown settled on his face as he rode down to the lobby of the medical building. He'd missed Mardi Gras. He'd really looked forward to taking Josie to the parades and having a good time. He needed to call Jack Emery, too. Hell, he needed to do a lot of things. First and foremost, though, he had to arrange an appointment with the private detective he'd hired to find his niece and her father. Tonight he was going to call André Haffauir and have him stop by the apartment for a long talk. He would order Chinese and they could settle up some business. Tomorrow, if nothing went awry during the night, he would head for New Orleans. He wanted to see Josie Dupré almost as much as he wanted to see Zip. Maybe more.

The ride uptown to his apartment was uneventful. Paul spent the forty minutes thinking about all the decisions he'd made during the last ten days. He hoped he was doing the right thing. Maybe the mugging in the park had been a good thing in a cockamamie kind of way. It made him reassess his life to date and to plan what he was going to do with his future. "Life is just too damn short," he mumbled. His shoulders these past ten days were lighter, so light at times that he felt giddy with relief. "I should have done this years ago."

"Six bucks, mister," the cab driver said.

Ten minutes later, Paul was writing out a check to one Hilda Klausner, a broad smile on his face. At the last second he pulled a crisp fifty dollar bill from the stash he kept in a drawer in his study and handed it to the weary nurse's aide who had accompanied him home. "Buy something special for yourself," he said kindly. For the first time he really noticed her rough red hands and the tired slump to her shoulders. If he remembered correctly, one of the candy stripers had said Hilda was a single mother with three children. "Ooops, hold on, Mrs. Klausner. I meant to give you this." He took back the fifty dollar bill and pulled out three one hundred dollar bills. "I also want to apologize if I was too cranky during your stay. I've never been confined like this before. Thank you for your excellent care."

The nurse's aide looked at the three one hundred dollar bills, her eyes filling with tears. Her large thick arms reached out and before Paul knew what was happening, he was engulfed and crushed to her ample bosom. "Your mother must be very proud of you, Mr. Brouillette. She raised a good son. If you need me for anything, here's my phone number. Take care of yourself, don't overdo it, and if you get tired, rest. Go easy on the caffeine and get a good night's sleep. I'll remember you in my prayers. Good-bye."

Paul sighed when the door closed behind Hilda. He almost missed her. He sniffed the stale air in the apartment. He decided he preferred perfume—Josie Dupré's perfume.

Drink in hand, settled in his recliner, Paul reached for the phone. The first number he dialed was Josie's. He frowned when the recording came on. He spoke briefly, inviting her to dinner the following evening. The second call was to Jack's private number. Again he heard a recording. He left a second message, wondering if it was remotely possible that Jack and Josie were together somewhere. His third call was to the airlines, and he booked his flight for noon of the following day. His next call was to the private detective, and he arranged a meeting for the middle of the week. The final call was to André Hoffauir, inviting him to dinner. "I want to see you, André. I'll order Chinese and some of the dark beer you like. We'll be working late, so don't make any plans for later on. I'll be leaving tomorrow for home. I want everything settled when you leave here tonight. I'll see you at seven."

Paul spent the next several hours showering, changing into sweats, and going through files in the study. He packed his briefcase, his garment bag, and a small carry-on bag. He carried all the cases to the door and set them down, after which he stretched out on the sofa, clicked on the television to CNN, and promptly went to sleep—something he'd never done in the whole of his adult life. He slept deeply and peacefully. The last time he'd slept deeply and peacefully was when he had been a small child.

He knew it was a dream because his mother had never visited his apartment in New York, nor had Josie Dupré, and yet they were both standing in his kitchen and they were fighting over him. He watched from the doorway, wondering why they didn't see him or the lady in the pink dress who smelled like a flower garden. He listened, a smile working at the corners of his mouth as his mother argued with the young caterer. He looked toward the doorway leading into the dining room to see if the lady in the pink dress was enjoying the dialogue as much as he was, but she was nowhere in evidence. That alone convinced him he was dreaming.

"My son can't marry you, chère, because he is married to the family business. He is the firstborn son, and it is his duty. I am his mother, and I know of what I speak."

Hands on her hips, her eyes sparking, Josie Dupré leaned toward Marie Lobelia. "I am the woman who loves him. He loves me. I have his dog. I love his dog. You wouldn't let Paul have a dog when he was little. He has one now, and he isn't going to give him up. I go with the dog. We all belong together. He took me to see Butterfunck! If you loved him, you'd let him go. You're his mother! My mother was the sweetest, kindest, most wonderful mother in the world. All she ever wanted was for Kitty and me to be happy. I never got to say good-bye to her. I will regret that for the rest of my life. You can make things right for Paul. Be the mother he always wanted."

"Bravo! Bravo!"

Paul rolled over on the couch, his head and neck drenched in sweat. Why in the hell was the lady in the pink dress shouting bravo? He ground his teeth when he focused his gaze on the television screen to hear one of the anchors shouting. He bolted upright. What the hell kind of dream was *that*? He wasn't certain, but he rather thought he smelled lilies of the valley.

The bar at the far end of the living room beckoned. He fixed himself a stiff scotch and soda. He gulped at the icy drink. He hated dreams because they made him think about his past.

Paul finished his drink and fixed a second one. He was almost finished with it when André Hoffauir rang the bell. His mood was expansive when he opened the door.

André was short and squat, a soccer ball of roundness. He had bright blue eyes that sparkled behind wire-rim glasses, and he wore a perpetual smile. "What are we celebrating, Paul?" he asked, tossing his jacket and the files he brought with him onto a bench in the foyer.

"My freedom and your shackles. I think it calls for a toast."

"Are we talking about what I think we're talking about?" André queried.

"You bet," Paul said. "I'm turning the business over to you. My mother will probably fight us in the beginning, but, hey, it's the way it has to be. There is absolutely no one else who can run the company or who wants to run it. You're it, buddy. I know you have plans for the different companies, and I know that you know how to implement them. You have my blessing. I'm going back to New Orleans to go into partnership with Jack Emery. You know I've wanted to do this from the day I graduated from college. Hell, it's all I ever wanted. Who knows, maybe I'll make a lousy architect. If I do, I'll find something else. I'm not coming back. Ever. We need to be clear on that."

"You're sure about this, Paul?"

"Hell, yes, I'm sure. For years you've ragged on me about getting married and raising a family. How could I do that when I'm so miserable and hate what I do for a living?"

"Are you saying you're going to get married?"

"Hopefully I will one of these days. I met someone. I want to be free to pursue a relationship. Do you understand, André?"

"Of course I understand. Listen, let's make some coffee for you before we start to talk business. Your mother and the aunts came to New York last week. They aren't happy. They were doubly unhappy when I told them you were unavailable. The cornmeal plant will be closed the first of June."

"No, we're not closing it. We're going to sell it and split the profits with the workers. That will take them past retirement. No one is going to get shafted. I'm working on something for my mother that I think will make her happy. It's just a matter of time."

"Are you listening to yourself, Paul? Who in the hell in their right mind would buy that archaic company? What kind of money are you talking about?"

"Me. I'm going to buy it. No one has to know that but you and me. Whatever it takes to do this is what I'll pay. You're in charge. Just don't leave a paper trail, okay?"

"You're talking some big bucks here, Paul."

"Yeah, I know. I'll sell this apartment, my stock, my entire portfolio. The whole ball of wax. If I have to, I'll sell the house in New Orleans. As I said, whatever it takes. How upset was my mother?"

"Did you ever see smoke coming out of someone's ears? She was breathing fire. But I had this weird feeling it was all an act, Paul. I think it was for the benefit of the aunts, who, by the way, didn't say boo."

"Did she make her usual threats?"

"No. I was prepared for anything she might throw at me. She gave up on that company a long time ago. I could tell. She goes through the motions, and that's it. It's a way of life. She knows it's operating in the red. I also told her it wasn't negotiable. Very kindly of course. I think I'd feel a lot better if you told me what your game plan is in regard to your mother."

Paul told him. "If we can find my niece and come to terms with my brother-in-law, I'm hoping she'll finally be happy and she won't begrudge my leaving. Maybe I'm fooling myself. It's the best I can do."

"Are you having any luck, finding any leads that look like they might pan out?"

"Right now they're looking up birth certificates. The detective seems to think my niece Nancy might have married and had children. He's trying to track her that way. You know, maiden names and all that. He seems hopeful, so that makes me hopeful. We'll find her—it's just a matter of when. I'm hoping for Mother's Day."

"I hope it works out. You ready to get down to work?"

"I will be as soon as we order dinner."

"Then let's get to it."

* * *

"Where are you going, Marie?" the aunts asked in unison.

"To the *jardin*. I need to think."

"Chère, are you going to think about *premier-né*?"

"My firstborn? No, June is gone. I gave up hope of ever seeing my granddaughter again. *Jamais*."

"Never ever is a very long time," the aunts said with one voice.

"Yes, it is. I need to sit quietly and think about my son, *homme de consequence*."

"If Paul is such a man of importance, then why is he closing the plant?" the aunts questioned.

"Because it is losing tons of money. It is a business decision. It must be. We can do nothing about it. Somehow, some way, he will make things right. I feel it here," Marie said, thumping her chest.

"Then why did we go traipsing into New York? We missed our programs for two days."

"We went because it was expected. It was the right thing to do. I voiced our objections. It no longer matters. Go, make some lemonade or sweet tea. I'll be in in a little while."

Marie knew they were watching her from the kitchen window, so she turned her chair around so they wouldn't see her tears. How was it that she was coming to the end of her life and was so bitterly unhappy? She had hoped against hope that Paul would be in the corporate offices when she got there. She'd had a speech all rehearsed—a careful speech in which she bared her soul and asked for forgiveness. For years now she had fought him tooth and nail for the cornmeal plant because it was the only communication they had. She could vent her anger at herself and him as well. All surface words that never got to the depth of the problem. *How could I have been so cruel, so stupid, to turn my back on my only son?* A boy who didn't understand. A young man who even today didn't understand what it meant to lose two daughters. She wondered what it would feel like to have her son throw his arms around her. To hear him say he loved her and mean the words. How wonderful that would be. She didn't deserve those things. In her heart and in her soul she knew those things would never happen. She cried softly into a scented lace handkerchief, her shoulders shaking with her grief.

Inside, the aunts huddled and whispered like magpies. Should they go to the *jardin* or should they stay inside and pretend they didn't know their beloved sister was crying her heart out? They decided to wait and watch because it was all they could do.

Josie's heart thudded and thumped as she listened to Paul Brouillette's message. The nerve! The unmitigated gall!

"That must have been some message," Kitty said. "You look like a scalded cat. In case you're interested, your hair is standing on end. Did someone cancel, or is it a monster party we can't handle? By the way, the new girl is working out great. Are you going to tell me who it was?"

"It was . . ." Josie sputtered. "It was *him!*"

Kitty clucked her tongue. "Him? That could be anyone, Josie. Do you mean Jack Emery, the diplomat, that screwball who was a race car driver or *the him?*"

"That's the one! Him!" Josie fiddled with the fringe on the place mats, her eyes wild. "He called, offered no explanations. Said he hoped Zip was okay and he would like to take me to dinner tomorrow night. It was a flat-out message."

Tongue in cheek, Kitty said, "Well that certainly explains why you look like such a wild woman. Guess you aren't going, huh?"

"Are you out of your mind? Of course I'm not going. Who does he think he is?"

Kitty giggled. *"Homme d'affaires* and *homme de consequence."*

Josie continued to pick at the fringe on the place mat. Her foot tapped the tile floor impatiently. "So he's a businessman and a man of supposed importance. So what!"

"You know you're going, so stop fussing. Let him wine and dine you and then tell him off. Tell him to take his dog with him. I'm tired of cleaning up his big poops. What are you going to wear?"

"Since I'm not going, I don't have to worry about that. Aren't you supposed to be loading the van or something?" Josie asked with an edge to her voice.

Kitty reached for the place mat and smoothed it out on the table. "I did. We have help now, you know. We're ready to go. I came in to get you since it's your turn to serve tonight."

"What did you make?"

"Snails and mugbugs."

"That's nice. Okay, I'm ready. I locked the dogs upstairs in the spare room."

"Is Jack Emery coming by later?"

"No, Jack Emery is not coming by later," Josie snapped. "What did you make again?"

"Fried quail eggs with pecan relish, crawfish stuffed pork chops with crawfish Bordelaise sauce, caramelized sweet potatoes and spinach coulis, banana cream pie and chocolate truffles."

"Interesting. I hope the bill is high."

"Sky-high. You were supposed to write it up, Josie. Did you do it?"

"If I was supposed to do it, then I did it. Stop being so grouchy, Kitty."

"I used to do crap like that when I was falling in love with Harry. I did all kinds of dumb things like forgetting to write up the bills, forgetting to do this or that, leaving out a key ingredient, etc., etc. So have you decided what you're going to wear?" Kitty giggled.

"The lemon yellow linen dress with my straw hat. The one with the rainbow-colored belt that matches my sandals."

"Good choice, Josie. Real good. Which perfume?"

"The sinful, decadent one."

"Way to go, girl! Make him lust after you. We have a whole batch of fresh mangos at home!"

"Save me two, okay?"

"You got it."

* * *

Jack Emery tossed his briefcase and jacket on the sofa. He headed straight for the kitchen, where he popped open a bottle of Corona beer. The phone rang just as he took his first swig.

"Jesus, don't tell me it's Paul Brouillette in the flesh. Where in hell have you been, you son of a gun? Do you have any idea what you put me through with that disappearing act? What the hell is going on?"

"I'm ready to sign on with you. I'm a free agent. I'll be home tomorrow afternoon. How's Zip?"

"How the hell should I know how your dog is? Fat with big feet and wild hair? I'm gonna get you for that one. Your lady friend has Zip. He rammed through the door when I went to get him. I had to buy a new screen door. I heard you had to go that route yourself. I took her to dinner. Let me be the first to tell you that you are not on the lady's top ten list. I think she more or less hates your guts right now. You got some major sucking up to do, buddy." He paused. "You really coming aboard, Paul?"

"Yeah, I am. Do I need to duck when I go over there?"

"Full body armor might do it," Jack guffawed. "By the way, we went to see Butterfunck. You might take her there again. It's just a suggestion. She does like to hoot and holler!" He stared at the pinging phone and laughed until tears rolled down his cheeks.

Jack swigged from his beer bottle. Hot damn, the big Cajun was finally seeing the light and coming aboard. That meant more free time, more vacations, and his best friend working right alongside of him. It didn't get much better than that. "I think, Miss Josie Dupré, you had something to do with all of this, and I do sincerely thank you."

Dressed in a custom-tailored suit, a pristine white shirt, and a designer tie, his hair slicked back, Jack Emery led his entourage into the New Orleans Airport. "You guys got it right now? The minute we see him you start playing 'When the Saints Go Marching In,' the girls throw the Mardi Gras beads, the photographer shoots, and you," he said, pointing to a scantily clad model, "hold up the champagne and your pals hold the wineglasses. We can drink it in the three stretch limos on the way to the office. Everybody set? You all know what he looks like, so let's get ready. Remember now, we parade out of here like we own the place, and for today we do. Sort of. Just keep playing 'Saints' until we get to the limos. This guy is going to be so dumbfounded he won't be able to utter a word," Jack said, smacking his hands together gleefully. When it came to Paul, it was always one-upmanship. He could hardly wait to find out how his buddy would retaliate. Whatever he did, it would be good.

"Okay, here come the passengers. There he is! Hit it, guys!"

Paul Brouillette's jaw dropped as strobes lit up. His eyes searched the crowd for some sign that all this was for him. His jaw dropped further when the scantily clad model threw her arms around him, a champagne bottle clutched in each hand. He felt a wet kiss on his check before his gaze locked with Jack's. Then he grinned. "It's a party!" he shouted, to be heard over the musicians.

"Damn straight, it's a party! It's all for you, buddy. There's another one going on at the office right now. It was the least I could do for my old buddy! Welcome home, Paul!" Jack said, clapping him on the back.

"Where's Zip?" Paul shouted.

"With the fat lady who has big feet. I'm gonna get you for that one!"

"Can we stop and pick him up on the way? I really missed him."

"I tried earlier, but no one was home. I didn't hear Zip bark, and I didn't want a repeat of that other night when he went through the door. We can pick him up after the party. It will only last an hour or so. We got some new guys at the firm, and they're dying to meet you. I also want to present your first job to you. Then, I'm going on vacation with Marissa."

"You're leaving me alone with . . . everything?"

"Hey, you're a partner now. You gotta jump in some time. Might as well be right away. You can handle it. If you screw up, so what? That's how you learn."

The sudden silence was deafening the moment the musicians started to pack up their instruments. Paul took off his jacket, rolled up the sleeves of his shirt, and yanked at his tie.

"See, you got it down." Jack laughed as he pushed his friend into the limo. "This one is just for us. The others go in the two behind us. Now, cut the bullshit and tell me about Miss Josie Dupré. Is it going to go somewhere? What can I do to help move things along? You'll never starve—that's for sure. Here," he said, handing over a bottle of champagne to Paul. He kept one for himself. Both corks popped simultaneously.

Paul swigged from the bottle. It was time to talk. Time to open up. Time to lighten his shoulders. It was time.

Eight

Kitty Dupré paced the long, narrow test kitchen, her face a mask of fury. "I've been cooking for eight straight hours and now you tell me the Larsens are canceling. Why? Who's paying for all this?" she exploded.

"Calm down, Kitty. Emma Larsen dropped off a check twenty minutes ago. We aren't out one cent. What we have is a ton of food. We can either eat it or take it to one of the homeless shelters. It's no big deal. If you want me to drop it off, I will. Then I have to get ready for . . . to . . ."

"I can see where you have a narrow window of only four hours," Kitty said. "I used to need at least six hours when I had a date with Harry. I'll package some of this up and take it up to the house in case you want to, you know, dine in. I'm staying at Harry's tonight. He's due in any minute now. We have two whole days We have a free day tomorrow, so I won't see you till Thursday. If you need me, call. Jill and I will drop the rest of this food off at the shelter. Go on, do your thing. The mangos are on the kitchen table."

Josie threw a wooden spoon at her sister, her face flaming.

Kitty laughed and laughed. "C'mon, sis, the guy's a stiff. He takes himself way too seriously. He needs to lighten up. Think of all the fun you could have if you'd both loosen up. Mom would tell you to go for it. She snagged Daddy with some rather unorthodox methods. Think about it." She struck a pose, reached for the rolling pin and held it in front of her as she started to sing.

I'm getting rid of all my pantyhose,
And all those high heels with the pointy toes.
I'm gonna find myself some comfortable clothes
I'm getting rid of all my pantyhose.
Now who decided what I'm supposed to wear?
Lots of makeup and all that big hair.
I've got a layer I've gotta expose.
I'm getting rid of all my pantyhose.

Josie burst out laughing as Kitty rolled her eyes as well as the rolling pin, pretending she was on stage. She strutted the length of the kitchen to Josie's delight.

"Enough! That song has been buzzing in my brain since the day you bought that Corinda Carford CD."

"Do you think I have the makings of a songbird?" Kitty laughed.

"You are no Corinda Carford—that's for sure. So don't quit your day job."

"Don't forget what I told you about the mangos. They're soooo ripe."

"One nutcase in the family is enough. If you're sure you don't need me, then I have things to do. You could drop the Larsens' check off at the bank on your way to the shelter. It's on my desk, along with the deposit slip. We need to send some flowers. Mr. Larsen is in traction at the hospital. He slipped on some soapsuds in the laundry room. I guess he lay there in agony until his son came in from school. He'll be fine, though."

"I'll order the flowers. Where are the dogs?"

"In the kitchen. I'll keep them with me."

Josie galloped up to the house, her heart thumping in her chest. She was going to see Paul in a few hours. A good, long soak in a bubble bath. A manicure and a pedicure were definitely called for. She needed to shave her legs, and she definitely needed to do something with her hair. Four hours to ground zero. Four hours until Paul Brouillette walked through her kitchen door. She closed her eyes and whirled around the kitchen. Both dogs followed her every move, as she twirled the dishtowel this way and that, a dreamy look on her face. She stopped for a minute and picked up one of the mangos from the bowl on the kitchen table. No way. Never in a million years. Kitty was right: They were so ripe. Another day and they would be rotten. So much juice. So delicious. She could almost feel the warm, sticky juice dripping down between her breasts. Almost.

"Let's go, guys. Time to get gussied up. Time is marching on, and your owner will be visiting very soon, Zip. Hop to it!"

Both dogs bounded out of the kitchen and up the steps, where they waited, panting for her to get to the top. When she reached the top, they raced down the hall to her bedroom. Zip always took a flying leap and landed smack in the middle of the bed while Rosie had to climb on the little bench Josie had placed at the foot of the bed to make it easier for her to get up and down.

The boxer eyed the wild array of clothing on the bed. He sniffed and pawed everything until he cleared a space for himself and Rosie. One huge paw reached out to an undergarment that was little more than cobwebs and lace. He dangled it over the side of the bed. "Is that a yes or a no?" Josie giggled as she took the teddy and carried it to the bathroom.

"Woof."

Water gushed into the old-fashioned tub with the claw feet as Josie eyed the array of bath salts in crystal decanters on the shelf over the tub. Honeysuckle, lavender, avocado, lily of the valley, rose hyacinth. She reached for the lily of the valley and poured lavishly. "You're here, aren't you, Mom? I can feel your presence. Maybe it's wishful thinking on my part. Yes, I can talk to Kitty, and yes, she gives me good advice. Most of the time. It's you I want to talk to. God, I wish you were here. I like this guy. Probably more than I should. He could be *the one,* Mom. He really could. Kitty's right: He is rather stiff. Reserved. I see pain in his eyes. I know that sounds stupid, but it's there. I can feel that pain the way I can feel you're close by. I want to do everything right tonight. I want him to want to see me again. Not because of the dogs but because of me. Maybe there's something I should do to let him know how I feel. Maybe I should say something. How dressed up should I get? What if I get dressed up and he's casual? What if he's *duded* up to the nines and I'm casual? I never get it right, Mom. I feel so alone. I don't know why that is. Did I ever tell you I was sorry about the time I snatched your pearls and broke them? That's what I mean, Mom. I never got to say so many things. I wanted to. I loved those pearls. I know how much those pearls meant to you because Daddy gave them to you for your first anniversary. You didn't even get mad. You said you always felt warm and loved when you wore them. You didn't punish me; you didn't whip my ass. I never understood that. I did write you a letter, though, but I didn't give it to you. I'm sorry, Mom. Did you know I cried buckets for days when you gave me pearls for my seventeenth birthday? I wrote you a letter about that, too. I'm not going to do that mango thing, though."

Josie stopped her monologue long enough to shed her clothes and pour a glass of wine, which she carried to the tub. A fifty-minute soak was going to work wonders.

Ground zero was thirty-five minutes away when Josie added the last pin to the French twist. She peered into the mirror. Stray tendrils of hair curled about her forehead and ears. There was nothing she could do about them, so she let them be. She reached for the perfume bottle, spritzed the air, and danced under the spray. Delicious. Absolutely delicious.

Something was missing. The yellow linen was plain, but perfect. The sandals were just right. If she didn't sit down for the next thirty-five minutes she would be fine. She loved linen, but it did wrinkle. "What do you think, guys? I need something. I don't feel *finished.*"

Rosie circled her feet, trying to lick the lotion on her ankles. Zip romped across the room to widen the circle behind Rosie and in doing so bumped into the organdy-skirted dressing table, upending the little bench Josie sat on to apply her makeup. She watched as her jewelry box tilted and fell open, the contents scattering on the glass vanity table. A single strand of pearls floated to the floor.

Josie whirled around, her arms outstretched as she moved about the room in a crazy wild dance, the dogs behind her. "Mom!" When there was no response—and she knew there wouldn't be—Josie dropped to her knees to pick up the pearls, knowing the yellow linen was going to be wrinkled when she got up. She didn't care. Instead, she fastened the pearls around her neck. She wanted to cry so bad she bit down on her lower lip to stem the flow of tears. She wondered if anyone would believe her if she told them her mother was there. Kitty might. Then again, maybe not. Either you believed or you didn't.

She believed.

Paul's head buzzed as he shook hands all around. He couldn't remember ever feeling as good as he felt right then. Everyone seemed genuinely glad he was aboard. He was going to like working there, doing something he loved. Finally. It was his day. A day he thought would never arrive, but it had. Thanks to a mugging in Central Park.

Another round of good-byes, and then Jack literally pushed him out the door. "I'm taking you home, buddy, and you're going to chug down a pot of coffee before you meet the lady with the big feet. You don't want her bouncing you out on your ear. Besides, you said the private dick was coming by at five. It's almost five now. Let's get this show on the road."

"Sounds like a plan to me. Where do you think I should take Josie for dinner?"

"I think, if I were you, I'd try to coax her into cooking something for you. Stay in, cuddle on the couch, and don't drink any more. You like this little gal, don't you?"

"Yes, I do," Paul said smartly.

"You don't have a good track record with women. Do you want some advice?"

"No, I do not want any advice. I can handle my own love life. You haven't done that well yourself."

"That's true," Jack said amiably. "You, on the other hand, are a different story. You just love 'em and leave 'em."

"That's also true, but I've been in no position to get serious about anyone. My life has been at odds, and I could never subject a woman to something like that. It wouldn't have been fair. Now that I've shed my shackles, I'm free to pursue a relationship."

"Are you going to go to see your mother?"

"Eventually. I really don't want to talk about that right now, Jack."

"By the way, Paul, you can take Zip to the office with you if you want. He'll make a good mascot. There will be no end of people to walk and play with him. We run a loose ship. It's something to think about. Okay, we're home. Do you want me to come in and make you that pot of coffee?"

The look Paul shot at his friend was so withering, Jack flinched. "I think I'm capable of making my own coffee and drinking it, too. Thanks, buddy. Pick up your lady and have a great time. I'll see you when you get back. Were you serious about me taking Zip to the office?"

"Yep. I love that big hound. See ya, buddy."

Paul unlocked the door and walked into his house, aware of the thundering silence. He looked around at the perfection the decorator had created as though seeing it for the first time. He threw his tie on one chair, his jacket on another. He stood back, took a basketball stance and pitched his briefcase in the general direction of the couch. It landed on the hearth. He threw back his head and howled with laughter. The garment bag and carry-on bag were shoved to the middle of an exquisite Oriental rug. He laughed again when the rolled-up newspaper worked loose from the flap on the carry-on bag and toppled to the floor. He gave it a kick and watched the paper spread in all directions. All he needed was for Zip to be there to poop on the paper.

He walked from room to room, wondering why his house still smelled like paint and wallpaper paste. He hated the smell almost as much as he hated the smell of a new car. He made his way to the back of the house, stopping in the kitchen to grab a chicken leg and a hunk of cheese. He backed up, filled the coffeepot, poured water, swung the basket to the left, and listened to the machine grind the beans. When it swung back into place he moved on to the room he shared with Zip. Not that Zip was confined to that one particular room. He had the run of the house but seemed to like the glassed-in room the best. He could see outside and fantasize about catching the squirrels and geckos that climbed the trellis. What in hell was he going to do if Zip didn't want to be with him anymore? How was he going to handle that? Man and his dog. That was supposed to be the way it was. Now there were two females in his life, Josie and Rosie. He had to decide what he was going to do about *that,* too. He chomped on the chicken leg and wondered if he was falling in love. Whatever it was he felt for Josie Dupré, it was something he'd never felt for another woman. Therefore, it had to mean something. He needed to start paying attention to things like that.

Paul looked at his watch just as the front doorbell rang. The private dick! Punctual. Punctual was good. He gnawed on the chunk of cheese as he made his way to the front door. He felt so pleased with the mess in the living room, he gave himself a mental pat on the back.

The detective was big and burly, rather like a tree

trunk with four limbs. His hands were bigger than ham hocks. Paul wondered if his face showed any pain at the bone-crushing handshake. He wished he could soak his hand in hot water. "Let's go in the kitchen so you can spread out if need be. Can I get you a drink? Coffee, beer, soda pop?"

"Do you have any lemonade?"

"I don't know. I'll look. How about a sandwich, a chicken leg or some ham and cheese," Paul said, ripping a chunk of ham off the plate. He stuffed it into his mouth. "I think this is lemonade in the pitcher. Want to try it and see? My housekeeper must have made it." The detective nodded as Paul whipped out a glass and poured. "So, whataya got?" he said as he fixed coffee for himself.

"What I have, Mr. Brouillette, is so hot I'm afraid to talk about it. I think I found your brother-in-law and your niece. They're living in Lafayette. I was right about your niece. She has a little boy named Peter. The father changed their name when they moved. That took some tracking. By the father I mean your brother-in-law. They've been going by the name of Tullier. Your niece must have a streak of independence in her because she listed her mother's maiden name on the child's birth certificate. By the way, she isn't married."

Paul waved that aside as being of no consequence. "Are they well? Do they need anything?"

"They live in a small apartment. It looks clean and tidy. The little boy is dark-haired and dark-eyed. Sturdy. He has a speckled dog he plays with in the yard. It's fenced in. They certainly aren't rich if that's what you want to know. Your niece works as a private secretary at a law firm and the boy goes to day care during the day. She drives an eight-year-old Honda. Your brother-in-law works as a security guard at one of the hotels. I spent days of surveillance on the two of them, so I have their routine down pat. Your brother-in-law has a heavy-duty gambling problem. He probably drinks more than he should, too. I think your niece pretty much supports herself and the boy. They had no clue they were being watched. You can go there anytime. I can go with you if you want, even though my job is finished. I'm sorry it's taken me so long to get results for you. We can settle up now or I can bill you. Good lemonade."

"I'll get my checkbook. I don't suppose you took any pictures."

"Yes, sir, I took two rolls of film. Zoom lens. Everything is in the folder."

Paul could hardly wait for the detective to leave. He scribbled out the check and ushered him to the door so fast the man thought his feet had sprouted wings. "Thanks for all your hard work."

"Good luck, Mr. Brouillette."

Paul nodded. He literally ran to the kitchen, where he ripped open the folder. His eyes burned when he stared down at the little boy sitting on a rusty tricycle. But it was the picture of his niece that allowed the tears in his eyes to escape. She looked so much like his sister it was uncanny. His mother was going to be so happy. Hell, he was happy.

Happier than he'd been in years. His gaze strayed to the little boy with the speckled dog. "He's a Brouillette," he chortled happily. "By God, he's a Brouillette."

Paul leaned back in his chair. His cup was full to the brim. Life was suddenly so wonderful he wanted to shout and dance and do all the things he'd never done as a kid. All you had to do was persevere. If you did that, you prevailed. He was the living proof. "Thank you, God," he said, bowing his head.

Paul closed his eyes. His heart told him to go to Lafayette in the morning. His head said wait until the weekend. Maybe Josie Dupré would go with him. Women knew about things like this. Her presence might convince his niece to return with him. He certainly didn't want to scare his niece in any way. Women were so protective of their children. Yes, the weekend was the best solution. He certainly didn't want to leave his new firm the first day on the job. Jack wouldn't mind, but he still wasn't going to do it. Besides, he needed a few days to think it through, to plan, to hug this news to his chest. After all this time, after all the near misses, the long months and years of searching. His mother was going to be so happy. He could see her face now. Peter. Strong name. Peter Brouillette. Little Pete. Petey. And a speckled dog. A whole little family. He would be Uncle Paul. He felt his chest puff out.

Paul looked at the kitchen clock. Time to shower and shave. He should probably make a dinner reservation somewhere. He stopped in his tracks when he remembered

Jack's words: *Ask her to cook something for you.* Eggs would be good. He liked eggs at any time of the day. He wouldn't have to get dressed up. Jeans and loafers. Zip would be all over him; dog hairs would settle. Yeah, yeah, jeans and loafers. Tomorrow he could take Josie someplace special. She wouldn't mind. That was one of the things he really liked about her. She was agreeable. And nice. Real nice. Really, really nice. And he liked her. Liked her a lot. He really did. If things worked out right tonight, he would tell her just how much. Damn! Life was looking so good he crossed his fingers that nothing would go wrong.

Showered, shaved, hair combed, and dressed in jeans, a Gap T-shirt and loafers, he was ready to go with forty minutes to spare. He settled himself in the recliner and clicked on the television. He watched as Vanna White turned the letters. He closed his eyes and was asleep in seconds.

Paul bolted out of the recliner when he heard his mother's grandfather clock in the foyer chime eleven times. He looked at his watch in horror. "Shit!" he said succinctly.

He slammed through the house and galloped down the street, around the corner and up the Dupré driveway. He leaped over the picket fence like he'd been doing it for years. There she was, sitting on the back steps under the porch light and she looked, as Jack would say, pissed.

"Ah, Josie. Hey, it's me, Paul."

"Ah, Paul. Hey, it's me, Josie."

"Look, I'm sorry . . ."

"Save your sorry excuses for someone who cares. Did we or did we not have a date for eight o'clock?"

"Yes, we did, but you see . . ."

Josie stood up. "Do you see this dress? At seven-thirty it was wrinkle-free. It's now eleven-fifteen and it looks like a dishrag. I spent all last night ironing it. It took me hours. It takes a long time to iron linen. I've had it with you, Mr. Brouillette. Take your damn dog and go home. Don't call me again and don't bring your dog here either. You know what you can do. You can just kiss my . . . my . . ."

"Your what?" Paul drawled. He was so close he could smell her breath and the other delicious scents emanating from her body. He leaned even closer and lowered his head. In the whole of his life he had never experienced such gentle passion. His knees turned to rubber and he held on to her. When she gasped, he drank in air and kissed her again. When his legs gave out, he lowered her to the step without unlocking his lips from hers. When he finally came up for air, he was the one who gasped.

"Oh, do that again."

"I can't. I feel like Gumby. Lady, you are one wild kisser."

"I know," Josie said sweetly. "What's your excuse? I also want to know why you dumped your dog on me."

"It's a very long story. I mean it's really long. I'm hungry. Do you think you could make me some eggs? You aren't mad anymore, are you? Where's my dog?"

"Your dog is sleeping on my bed with the door closed. He loves me, you know. I don't think he's going to want to go with you."

"That's what you think. That's my dog. He goes where I go. He might love you, but he loves me more. I've had that dog since he was a pup. He's mine."

"Then go upstairs and get him. Tell him you're taking him home. He'll do that under-the-bed thing again. Give it up—he's mine now. He loves Rosie, and he won't leave without her."

"Then there's only one thing to do."

"You aren't taking Rosie, so don't even think about it."

"Marry me."

"Marry you! I don't even know you. Why would I want to do a dumb thing like that?"

"Because it's the only solution. That way both dogs will be happy. You kissed me like you knew me. And," he drawled, "you invited me to kiss your ass. That's pretty personal if you want my opinion."

"I didn't say . . ." Josie sputtered.

"You were going to say it. You were hopping mad. You were right to be mad. I'm sorry. I can apologize from now till tomorrow, but it won't change things. Today was a day to end all days. I sat down, closed my eyes, and then it was eleven o'clock. I'm sorry about your dress. Where'd you get it, Taiwan?"

"No, I did not get it in Taiwan. I bought it in a very exclusive store in town and paid a lot of money for it. It looked nice at seven-thirty."

"You should ask for your money back." Paul grinned as he headed for the steps. "Are you going to feed me or not?"

"Why don't I ever win with you?" Josie grumbled.

"Because your heart isn't in it. You like me, admit it. Are you going to marry me or not?"

Josie looked around the kitchen, at the open door and windows. The scent of lilies of the valley was so strong she felt faint. Her fingers clutched at the pearls around her neck. *You trying to tell me something, Mom?* "If I agree to marry you, will you be on time for the wedding?"

"I'll go to the church the day before and wait. Are you saying yes?"

"I think so. I think my mother wants me to marry you. That has to be what it means. Okay, yes."

"You can explain that to me later. I want to see my dog. Rustle up some food, woman. I'm starving."

"You can't order me around. Don't even go down that road."

"Josie, do you think you could possibly find me something to eat?"

"That's much better. I'll try."

The minute he was out of sight, Josie twirled around. "Mom, where are you? You wanted me to say yes, right? I said yes. I wanted to say yes. It's a good thing, right, Mom? Please, give me a sign. Something. I need to know, Mom."

She heard them on the stairs, the man she'd just agreed to marry and the two dogs. Zip let out an earsplitting bark that sent Josie's hand to her throat and the pearls around her neck. She watched in delight as the necklace broke and the tiny circles rolled across the floor. She laughed happily as she dropped to her knees to pick them up. She was still laughing when Paul dropped to the floor across from her.

"Why are you laughing, Josie? You just broke your necklace. I'll buy you a new one."

"I don't need a new one. I don't want one either. Someday I'll tell you what this means."

"Promise?"

"Yes, I promise." *Thanks, Mom.*

Zip nuzzled Josie's neck and tried to inch her toward the door. "He wants out."

"Really."

"Yes, they've been cooped up since seven-thirty. I'd let them out if I were you. Otherwise, you're going to be cleaning up a mess. I'll put dinner in the oven."

"You cooked!"

"Our client slipped and fell on some soapsuds and the food was all prepared. Kitty took most of it to a homeless shelter, but I kept some in case we decided to eat here."

"So what are we having?" Paul called over his shoulder as the dogs raced into the night.

"We are having a salad of new potatoes and roasted walnuts with warm bacon vinaigrette, beef tenderloin with fresh horseradish and black-pepper crust, an exotic mushroom bread pudding, fresh cranberry compote, and a creole trifle."

"You did all that? I'm impressed."

Josie demurred. "I didn't . . ."

"I know it was for someone else but, hey, I'm getting it. So as far as I'm concerned, you did it for me. Are you going to cook like this every day when we get married?"

"No."

"I can understand that. In a business like yours you wouldn't want to cook after working all day. We'll hire a cook and housekeeper." He was getting married. He'd just asked the woman sitting on the floor to marry him. Was he of sound mind? Maybe this would be a good time to tell her about getting mugged and his concussion. And, if he was getting married, he needed to tell her about his past and his future. "While our dinner is warming up, I'd like to talk to you, Josie. There are some things you need to know about me. I'd like to get it all out in the open right now. If you want to change your mind, I'll understand. Let's have some wine and sit out on that little porch where your office is."

Josie felt a lump form in her throat. He sounded almost ominous. A chill raced up and down her spine. She reached for a bottle of wine and two glasses on the counter. Confessions were not for the weak of heart. He was right, though: Now was the time to get it all out in the open. She'd let him go first.

It was a beautiful evening, warm and fragrant. Overhead, stars winked and glistened as Josie walked along. It felt wonderful. She wished she could cross her fingers, but she was holding the wine bottle, and the two glasses were in her other hand.

Paul talked steadily as he uncorked the wine. He poured generously. Josie listened, her heart hammering in her chest. She heard his pain, felt it right along with him. At one point, she reached out for his hand and squeezed it. He squeezed back. She let her head drift to his shoulder. When his hand reached up to touch her hair, she felt like crying.

"That's pretty much it in a nutshell. I was wondering if you would like to go to Lafayette with me on Saturday. I'm prepared to bring my niece and the boy back if they want to come. I thought they could stay at my house until I decide how to handle it with my mother."

"I'd love to go with you if you're sure I won't be in the way. Where does your mother live?"

"In the French Quarter. She lives there with her sisters. She was managing the cornmeal plant, but we're selling it. I'm hoping this is all going to work out right. If it doesn't, I don't know what I'll do. That's why I came to you the first time. I wanted to plan a Mother's Day party for my mother. I was hoping against hope that we would be able to find Nancy in time for the party. In a way it's a trade-off. At least I think that's the way my mother is going to look at it. I've done this every year for years, hoping it would work out. It never did until now."

"What . . . what's your mother's name, Paul?"

"Marie. Why?"

"I've been working with her. She, too, wanted to plan a party for her sisters." She told him about her visit to the French Quarter and the walled-in garden and about the sisters coming to work for a few hours in the test kitchens. "She doesn't view it the way you do, Paul. She loves you very much. She's afraid to make advances to you for fear of rejection. She said you only call when you can fit her into your busy schedule. No woman—I don't care who she is—likes to be fitted in to someone's busy schedule. You need to sit down and tell her how you feel. She'll tell you how she feels, and then you will meet somewhere in the middle. If we're going to get married and have children, I want them to know their grandmother. I don't want to dance around my husband and make lame excuses. She's your mother, and you'll never have another. Trust me, I know what I'm talking about. You aren't one of those macho guys who can't admit you're wrong, or is too big to let your mother know how you hurt, are you?"

"No, I'm not one of those. How'd you get so smart?"

"I had a great mother. My dad was okay, too. If you let me, I can help."

"That's for tomorrow. Tonight is for us."

"I have news for you: It's tomorrow already. My watch says it's ten minutes of one. I'm kind of sleepy."

"Want to go to sleep?"

"Just like that, go to sleep?"

"Uh-huh. I turned down the bed when I was up there."

Josie doubled over laughing. "Then Zip is under the covers, and Rosie is on the pillow."

"Let's fake 'em out and head for the spare bedroom," Paul said, drawing her to her feet.

"What about dinner?"

"What about it?" Paul said lazily.

"Uh-huh. I'll just turn off all the burners and the oven."

"Sounds like a plan."

"Yes, it does. Do you think this night would have ended like this if you were on time?"

"Probably not. You need to get rid of that dress—it's a mess."

"Want to see me without it?" She heard him suck in his breath, or was that sound coming from her own mouth? "First door on the left!" Josie said, sprinting up the steps.

Nine

Josie woke slowly. She was instantly aware of where she was, of the warm body next to hers and everything that had transpired earlier. She smiled, then opened her eyes. Incredible dark eyes stared into hers. His smile matched her own. His voice was warm and husky when he said, "Good morning"

"This is the first time I've seen you look worry-free," Josie whispered softly.

"That's because tons of responsibility have shifted off my shoulders. You have a lot to do with it, Josie. Are we really going to get married?"

Josie's stomach fluttered in panic. "You did ask me. I remember saying yes. That was last night, though. I was a little hot under the collar, and you were chagrined, to say the least. If you want to renege, it's okay," she said lightly as she crossed her fingers under the covers.

"Not on your life. When?"

When indeed. "You have something to say about it,

Paul. Weddings take some time to prepare. Kitty is getting married in January. We could have a double wedding. Twins do things like that. Or we could go to a justice of the peace. I've never been married before, so I'm not sure what the rules are." With her index finger, Josie played with the dark curls drooping over Paul's forehead.

"That feels good. How are you at shoulder rubs?"

"Terrible. Unless of course we take turns. This has to be fifty-fifty all the way. We need to be clear on this, Paul."

"We are. What time is it? Where are the dogs?"

"It's seven-twenty and the dogs are outside the door. They've been whining for ten minutes. What time do you have to be at work?"

"Eight. I think. No one said. Do we have time . . . ?"

"'Fraid not," Josie said, swinging her legs over the side of the bed. She walked naked into the bathroom and closed the door. She heard Paul groan. She grinned from ear to ear as she brushed her teeth. She sashayed out of the bathroom five minutes later dressed in the worn, frayed, but comfortable robe that she'd had since she was sixteen.

"I'll let the dogs out and make coffee. Would you like toast or something?"

"Coffee will be fine. I have to go home and change my clothes. What should I do about Zip?"

"The same thing you've been doing every day since I met you—leave him here with me."

"I could move in. Or you could move in with me."

"I don't like your house, Paul. It's cold and unfriendly. You don't have any green plants or junk. I like *stuff*. You know, fill corners with things. Mementos. I like warm and cozy."

Paul slapped at his forehead. "You're right. That's what's wrong with the place. I threw stuff all over yesterday. I messed it up, and it still looked the same. Zip and I more or less lived in the family room off the kitchen. I guess it's a woman thing, huh?"

"More or less." That's what she could do today. With Kitty gone and no pending jobs, she could go to the French Market, buy some junk, some plants, and fix up Paul's house. She had the van, so she could shop till she dropped and load it to the brim. A labor of love. She literally danced down the steps behind the dogs. *It's going to be a wonderful day. I can feel it in every bone of my body.* "I'm getting married!" she shouted as she twirled around the kitchen, coffee strainer in hand. "Wherever you are, Mom, can you hear me? I'm getting married! Do you believe it, Mom? Me, getting married! Damn, I feel good. The pearls broke, Mom. That was my sign, right? I hope you approve of Paul. He's the one, Mom. I knew it the minute he showed up at the cottage. When you have time, give me another sign that you approve. You have to approve, Mom. I love this guy. I really do."

Paul backed away from the doorway. He hated to admit he had listened unashamedly to Josie's dialogue with her mother. She really did love him. No woman had ever said she loved him. Maybe his mother had told him she did when he was little, but if she did, he couldn't remember it. Maybe the old housekeeper had told him, too, but he couldn't remember that either. He felt his chest swell with happiness.

"How's the coffee coming?" he bellowed from the doorway.

"It's coming. Another minute or so. Are you going to make it on time?"

"Probably not. I'll say I thought I was to be in at eight-thirty. Hey, I'm a partner."

"What's your first project?"

"The guy is a new client for Jack. He wants a guest cottage, a cabana, and some interior renovations on his main house. I have to go over to the property this morning and then I get to sit down and see if I'm as good as I think I am."

"Trust me, you are. When someone wants something as bad as you've always wanted this, it has to work."

Paul nodded. "This is a pretty cup," Paul said, pointing to the large red strawberry. "That's what I mean. I don't have anything like this. My cups have a maroon stripe around the middle."

"They were my mother's dishes. There are only a few pieces left. Kitty and I treasure them. Growing up, food on a pretty plate made some things easier to eat, like liver or cauliflower. At least that's what Mom said. I have to agree. Kitty and I fight over them."

"Good coffee," Paul said, gulping from the cup. "I hate to drink and run, but I don't have any other choice. Hey, Zip!"

Josie watched, a smile on her face as Paul tussled with

the boxer for a few minutes. He raised his head to look at Josie. "Would you mind coming to my house for dinner with the dogs? I'd like to spend some time with Zip. I can barbecue outside if you like."

"Sure, I'd like that. What time?"

"How does seven sound? If I kiss you, I'll never get out of here."

Josie laughed. "Go on. I'll see you tonight."

The kitchen was suddenly quiet as Zip looked at the door, at her, and then at Rosie. He nudged his pal and both dogs crawled under the table.

"It's okay, Zip. We're going over there tonight, and you can show Rosie all your things and how you live. Paul and I will walk you guys and play with you all night. I promise. We're a package deal now. We all belong together. It's wonderful! It's so wonderful I feel like crying. I'm not going to cry, though. I will cry on my wedding day. My mother said she cried on hers, and then she never cried again. Well, she said she did cry one more time when Dad had his heart attack. She said she never let him see her cry, though. I have to remember that. Okay, time to shower and then we're going to the market. It's okay, Zip—really it is. We're going to your house to do some fixing up. Come on, give me some love," Josie said, rubbing her nose against the boxer's wet snout. "Ah, that's good. You too, girl. Kisses, kisses. Just one big happy family. The four of us. Please, God, don't let anything spoil all of this."

* * *

It was two-thirty when Josie pulled the van into Paul's driveway. She grinned from ear to ear as she surveyed her booty. She rather thought she'd bought everything under the sun. First things first. She opened the French doors and watched the two dogs barrel through the house, yapping and yipping at the tops of their lungs. She set down bowls of water before she started carrying her purchases into the house. The kitchen first. Always the kitchen, the heart of the home. She couldn't wait to tie the red-and-white-checkered cushions onto the ugly wrought-iron chairs. The moment she tied the last bow she knew she'd made the right choice. The checkered place mats with the matching napkins transformed the ugly glass-topped table to a work of art. The centerpiece of bright red ceramic apples in a straw basket complemented the mats and cushions to perfection. "Wonderful," she chortled.

Josie ran to the van for the pink tool kit that Kitty had given her for Christmas one year. In seconds she was standing on the kitchen counter screwing in an eye hook to hang a delicious fern, as big as a bushel basket, over the sink. "I love it, I love it, I love it!" She laughed at the dogs, who were sitting on their haunches watching her with interest. "That thing that looks like a bordello bedspread has got to go. What do you think of this?" she said, waving yards of red-and-white-striped sailcloth. "Let me tell you, this was a find! You see, you fit two rods into it and you have a canopy curtain." She banged more nails. What was it her father always used to say? Screw and glue. Well, she didn't have any screws or glue, so nails would have to do.

"Do you believe this!" she shouted to the dogs when she jumped down from the ledge. "Look, it's a whole different kitchen! No, not yet. The rugs!" She ran to the van again and carried in two braided rugs made of colored fiber. One went down in front of the sink and one in front of the stove. "I should have been a decorator," she said, tweaking Zip's ears. She stood back to survey her handiwork. "What we have here, ladies and gentlemen, is one hell of a cozy, warm kitchen. If there's even the remote possibility that I might be living here one day, I can handle this. I should have been a decorator. Maybe I missed my calling. Okay, onward and upward. Dining room and living room are next."

It was four o'clock when Josie called a halt to her decorating. She popped a Coke and sat down on the floor with the dogs. "Plants make all the difference. Some junk on the tables, some colored cushions, some flower arrangements, and the place looks lived in. I do like color. I think Paul likes it, too. Okay, guys, we can go home now. We're coming back later. Do you want to bring anything, Zip? Go get it, boy! No? Okay, let's head for home. Want a ride, Rosie?" she said, bending over to pick up the little dog. In a flash, Zip was between her and Rosie. He picked her up daintily and carried her out the door. Josie's vision blurred for a moment. Such devotion. "It's okay, baby. I understand." And she did understand. She really did.

Outside, the air was fragrant with the scent of lilies of the valley. Josie closed her eyes and inhaled deeply. She looked down at the flower border to see that all the tiny, fragile flowers had turned brown. She leaned over to pick one. There wasn't even the faintest scent emanating from the flower in her hand. "Thanks, Mom."

Paul had his jacket off before he hit the back door. He jerked at his tie, yanked it free, then slung it over his shoulder. He opened the door and blinked. Was he so tired he had walked into the wrong house? He craned his neck. No, this was his house. He stepped into the bright, cozy kitchen, his jaw dropping. He walked around, looking and touching everything, his eyes full of wonder.

He toured his house, his eyes getting wider and wider until he thought they would pop right out of his head. The whole place had been transformed. Everywhere he looked there were plants and bright, colored cushions. Knick-knacks were everywhere. He even had tassels and bell-pulls. Josie had done this. For him. For one incredible moment he thought he was going to burst wide open. The only room she hadn't touched was his and Zip's room. His sanctuary. No, she wouldn't touch that room. That alone told him everything he needed to know about Josie Dupré.

The doorbell pealed while he was standing in the middle of the living room. He opened the door and accepted the groceries he'd ordered. Wait till Ms. Josie Dupré found out what a good cook *he* was. He laughed all the way to the shower and was still laughing when he dressed in jeans and a T-shirt.

He opened a bottle of beer and sipped at it as he fired up the grill on the patio. He seasoned the steaks, then turned on the oven. He scrubbed the potatoes and vegetables. In less than an hour he had everything ready. All he had to do was set the table. When he opened the cabinets, he threw back his head and roared with laughter. He had new dishes decorated with luscious-looking fruit. His silverware had bright red handles, and his glasses were sky-blue. He sobered almost instantly. "Please, don't take this away from me. Please."

"Now this is what I call a perfect evening," Paul said as he dried the last dish and placed it in the cabinet. "You're staying, aren't you?" he said, wrapping her in his arms. "The dogs are asleep, and it would be a shame to wake them."

"Try and get rid of me," Josie said, lifting her lips to his.

"'Night, guys," Paul said quietly. Rosie squirmed out from her safe haven next to Zip and waddled over to Josie. Josie bent down to pick her up. She walked across the room with the little dog cuddled to her chest. She crooned and whispered to her. "I just want you to be happy, baby. It's okay—it really is. You'll always be my baby. Now I have Zip, too. Keep him in line. He's afraid I'm going to take you away from him. I would never do that. He just doesn't know it yet. You belong to me, and don't you ever forget it." The little dog licked at her face and then squirmed to get down. Josie swore later that the boxer nodded his satisfaction when Rosie stretched out alongside him. She watched, a smile on her face when she saw one big paw stretch out protectively.

"I guess our little brood is safe and sound."

"They're happy," Josie said with a catch in her voice. "My mother always said real, true love was making sure the other person was happy. I think she was right."

"Ha! I *know* she was right. I wish I had known your mother."

"I wish you had, too. She would have liked you. I think you would have liked her, too."

"You can use this bathroom. I'll use the one across the hall," Paul said.

"Okay." Josie turned around. "I love you, Paul Brouillette. I think you should know that."

"I love you, too, Josie Dupré. I think you should know that, too."

The wind outside the bedroom lifted, stirring the branches of the old oak tree, making it sway in an endless rhythm. The black night sky touched with stars was like a coverlet drawn over the old house when Paul turned off the lamp. They were alone, two souls, finding each other, getting to know each other all over again.

Naked together, they clung, kissing, murmuring, lips moving softly against lips. Her flesh came alive under his touch, her excitement and passion communicating with and stirring his own.

She was his love. He had held her this way before, just hours ago, worshiping at her breasts and taking possession of her innermost core, yet she excited and stirred him as if it were the first time. There was so much more to Josie than fair skin and alluring curves; there was the woman within, the woman he now knew he could not live without. He pulled her on top of him, wanting her to master their desire.

Wild blood coursed through her veins, her aching need for him cried within her soul. This was the man she loved.

Slowly he filled her with himself, and she opened to him, moving with him, imprisoning him in love's tender sheath. She whimpered softly, loving the feel of his body, responding to the sound of his tender whispers when he told her of her beauty and the way he loved the scent that was only hers.

He savored her lips, tasting the ambrosia of passion's fruit, tantalizing, withdrawing from her and entering again with slow, sensuous strokes and the caressing roll of his hips beneath her haunches. He inspired her to ride him, to take him deep within, helping her find the sweet fulfillment at the center of her being. His loving hands possessed her breasts, cupping their firmness, following their lovely slope to tease the pouting crests.

Fire sparked where their flesh joined, but it was only kindling to the raging conflagration of their souls. And when their lips met again, they tasted the salt of tears, and each thought it was their own.

Together they slept in one another's arms. And when they awoke in the early hours before dawn, they made love again and again.

Over coffee Paul leaned across his newly decorated table, his gaze locking with Josie's. He reached for her hand. "I don't know if I can wait till January or next year to get married. Why can't we get married now? Soon. Give me one good reason."

"I don't have a dress."

"Oh."

"A dress is important. It has to be just right. It has to say Josie Dupré is getting married in this one-of-a-kind dress. I would like my friends at my wedding. I'll have to track down a lot of them, as they move about. That takes time. Unless we have the wedding at your house or my house, we have to rent a hall. Usually they're reserved in advance. We'll need a caterer since I have no intention of catering my own wedding. August would be the earliest. Maybe July. No sooner. I don't want to get married on the fly and regret it later. I want it to be like my mother's wedding. If we start out right, then everything should fall into place for us. That's what my mother said, and I believed her then and still do. I'm no prude, but I can't move in with you either. I just can't do that. Do you understand?"

"Of course I do. I don't want you getting away from me."

"Look at me, Paul. Do you think for one minute I'm going to get away from you? No way. I found you, and I'm hanging on to you. We have two dogs to think about. Sleepovers are good."

Paul grinned. "Yes, they are. What's on your agenda for today?"

"Work. Kitty will be back. We have a cocktail party scheduled for late this afternoon. When that's over, we have to get ready for a champagne breakfast at the Rotary Club tomorrow morning. I won't be able to see you tonight."

"Then it works out. I have a meeting scheduled for six tonight that's going to run a couple of hours. How about dinner and a movie tomorrow night?"

"Not good. We have to spend more time with the dogs. How about if I rent some videos and I get Kitty to whip us up something at my house. Then the dogs and I will walk you home and we can start out early for Lafayette. Did you come up with anything in regard to your niece?"

"No. I'm just going to tell it to her the way I see it. I have a really positive feeling about it. I don't want to make any mistakes. I hope I'm doing the right thing by not telling my mother until I'm sure."

"If she doesn't want to come back with us, what will you do, Paul?"

"Then I'll tell my mother and explain her reasoning, whatever it may be. My mother can give her and her son a really good life. I hope she's mature enough to recognize and understand how important family is. I'm anxious about the meeting. I think seeing you with me will help a lot. By the way, my new client—my only client—doesn't like my ponytail."

"Oh pooh on him. I love it. You can tell him that, too. What is he, one of those ex-military guys with a buzz cut?"

"How did you know?"

"Just a wild guess. You'll be late if you don't hurry. I'll

lock up here and take the dogs to my house. I think they're getting the hang of it. They do love us, you know."

"How do you think they'll be with kids?"

Josie's heart fluttered. "I think they'll both be wonderful with kids."

"Then on that note, I'm leaving. I'm not kissing you good-bye today either."

Josie laughed. "'Fraidy cat."

"That's me."

"Go on before I make a lunge for you. I want your body! Go!"

Josie could hear him laughing all the way to his car. *God, I'm happy.*

"If this map the detective gave you is right, the apartment complex should be about a mile ahead. This rain is terrible. The weatherman said sunny and warm," Josie grumbled as she tried to peer through the driving rain.

"They never get it right. Maybe it's a good thing. You don't usually take a child out in rain like this."

"Do you know what you're going to do if your brother-in-law is home?"

"The detective said he works Saturday. That was another reason I wanted to wait until today. I called my mother yesterday from work, but she wasn't home. I just wanted her to know I was back in New Orleans although I'm sure André told her by now. I left a message, but she didn't return my call. Why is that, Josie?"

"She thinks you only call her when you have nothing

else to do or, as she put it, you fit her into your schedule. It's possible she was at the plant clearing out her things. André did tell her you were selling it, didn't he?"

"Of course he told her. Nicely and kindly. She went ballistic. We knew that would happen. I'm sure she's calmed down by now. In the end we had to think about all the other families who work for us in the other divisions."

"I'm sure she understands. She is, after all, a businesswoman."

"A seventy-four-year-old businesswoman. Her judgments are no longer sound. She lets her heart rule her head. That's not such a bad thing, but when it starts to affect the rest of the companies, then it's time to make hard decisions. It's a done deal, so there's no turning back. Is this the entrance?"

"Yes. Drive down to the second building, turn right, and it's building 4022. The apartment is on the first floor— 401. Do you want me to wait in the car?"

"Absolutely not. I'm just sorry you're going to get wet."

"Not to worry. I'll tie my hair up in a knot. Okay, let's make a run for it!" Holding hands, they sprinted from the car, slopping through puddles till they came to an overhang, where they checked the arrows with the printed apartment numbers. "This is it," Josie said, pointing to the apartment door to the left. Ring the bell, Paul."

Paul licked at his lips and rang the bell. A dog barked inside. The speckled dog in the picture.

She is pretty just like her mother, Paul thought.

"Nancy, I'm your uncle Paul Brouillette. This is Josie Dupré. Can we come inside? I'd like to talk to you. I can show you identification if you like." The young woman nodded. Paul opened his wallet and fished out his driver's license. She stared at it intently for a minute or so before she removed the chain from the door.

"Come in."

She's baking cookies, Josie thought. Probably for the little boy who was building a castle with colored blocks in the middle of the living room floor. The speckled dog hovered protectively.

"Let me wash the flour off my hands. Please, sit down. Would you like some coffee or maybe a soft drink?"

"We're fine," Paul said, his eyes on the dark-haired little boy. He had pictures of himself at the same age. *He looks just the way I did back then,* Paul thought.

She's so young, Josie thought. *And yet her weary eyes say she's seen more of the world than she wanted to see.*

"What do you want? My father isn't here," the young woman said bluntly.

"I know he isn't here. That's why I waited until today to come here. I've had a private detective looking for you. I came to take you home if you want to come with us. My mother—your grandmother—has never gotten over your mother's death. She would love for you to come home with your son. I would like to see you home with the family. How do you feel about that?"

"I guess I'm surprised," the young woman said quietly. "You didn't want us before. Why now?"

"Who told you a thing like that?" Paul demanded.

"My . . . my father. He said you all considered us baggage. He said we weren't wanted."

"No. No, no, that's all wrong. The day your mother was buried, your father packed up, took all her money, her jewelry, and you, and left. My mother tried for years to find you. She finally gave up. I didn't. We finally were able to locate you through the boy's birth certificate. Will you please come with us?"

"My father . . . Are you telling me the truth?"

"He's telling you the truth," Josie said quietly.

"I need to talk to my son."

Josie and Paul watched as Nancy walked over to her son and tapped him on the shoulder before she dropped down to eye level. Her fingers flew. The boy turned to look at them and smiled before he too used his fingers to communicate. They were signing. Josie heard Paul suck in his breath.

"Can't he hear?"

"Very little. He needs an operation and will have to wear hearing aids. We only have an HMO, and they don't want to pay for it. There just isn't any money left over for . . ."

"What about your father?" Paul said through clenched teeth.

"My father gambles and drinks a lot. For the most part, I have to support him, too. I have a good job, but the pay isn't that high. With day care I just can't afford it."

"The family will take care of it. Will you come with us?"

"You mean right now?" There was such hope in her face, Josie felt like crying.

"Right now, right this minute," Paul said gently. "Josie will help you pack."

"But my job . . ."

"We'll call your employer first thing Monday morning."

"My father . . ."

"We'll leave him a note and my phone number. He doesn't deserve even that, but we'll do it anyway," Paul said.

"The dog. The dog goes, too."

"You're absolutely right. The dog goes, too. I wouldn't have it any other way. What's his name?"

"Ollie. Pete named him. We found him alongside the road. I guess someone dumped him out of a car. I know what that's like."

"What about the boy's father?"

"He took off a week after Pete was born. He wasn't interested in responsibility or paying child support. We've done just fine without him. Should I call you Paul or Uncle Paul? What?"

"Paul will do just fine."

"I'll clean up the kitchen while you pack. Should I turn off the oven?" Josie asked.

"The cookies are done. Just take them out and leave the tray on top of the stove."

Paul inched his way over to the middle of the floor and sat down opposite the little boy. The speckled dog eyed him warily until he reached out to scratch him behind the ears. The little boy laughed. "Him likes that."

"I bet he does. How old are you, Pete?"

"Three. See, three fingers," he said holding up four fingers. Paul laughed. The little boy giggled.

Paul held out his arms. "C'mere." The detective was right. He was a sturdy, solid little boy, just the way Paul had been at the same age. He felt good in Paul's arms. Good and right. Hot tears pricked at his eyelids. "We're going to get you fixed up and you are going to have the best life there is. That's a promise." He held him away for a moment. "How would you like a bright red wagon and a new tri-cycle?"

The little boy's head bobbed up and down.

"We'll get Ollie a big ball and some toys and you can play in the same courtyard I did when I was little. Would you like that?"

"Mommie, too?"

"You bet."

"I'm ready," Nancy said.

"Do you have everything?" Paul said, appalled at the two suitcases.

"Yes, this is it. I wash a lot."

"You don't have to explain to us. Things will be different now. I promise you."

Nancy's fingers flew a second time. The little boy scampered out of Paul's lap. He gathered up the blocks into a box, then shoved it under a table.

"We're going with these people in the car. Ollie is coming, too. We're going to a new place to live where there are lots of trees and toys and little children for you to play with. This is your great-uncle Paul. And this lady is Miss Josie. Mind your manners now—you hear me?"

"Yes, Mommie."

"I'll come back for the bags. First we want to get settled in the car" Paul said.

Paul walked through the small two-bedroom apartment. He clenched his teeth at the single bed in the small room that also held a cot. Because of the clowns and animals on the spread, it was obvious the boy slept in the bed and Nancy slept on the cot. The bathroom was clean and tidy, the towels threadbare. "Damn!"

Something perverse in him made him march across the hall to the larger bedroom. It was messy and cluttered. Either it was hands-off, or Nancy didn't give a hoot about her father's room. He rather thought it was the latter.

The living room was small but clean. Three chairs, a coffee table full of cigarette burns, and a fifteen-inch black-and-white television. Other than the box of blocks under the table there was nothing else to see. At best, the furniture was worn, possibly secondhand. Hadn't he seen all this when he first walked in? No, he'd only had eyes for the little boy and his niece. What a colorless, flat existence. When his eyes started to burn again, he picked up the bags and closed the door behind him. He was never coming back there, and neither was Nancy, Pete, or Ollie.

Never.

Ever.

Ten

Kitty Dupré stared at her sister across the breakfast table. She knew immediately that there was something different about Josie. It wasn't just that she was staring out the window with a dreamy look in her eyes. She looked relaxed and at peace. Finally. She and her twin were so alike yet unalike in so many ways. Yes, they were tuned in to one another; yes, they thought alike on a variety of subjects; and yes, they wanted the same things out of life. Somehow, though, after their parents' deaths, Josie had never been the same. The shadows never quite left her eyes, and while she smiled, it always seemed like a practiced effort. So many times she'd bemoaned the fact that she didn't get a chance for that one last final good-bye. Life wasn't always fair, and sometimes life threw flyballs you were unable to catch no matter how hard you strained.

Kitty wished now that she had woken Josie when she got in last night, but it had been way too late, and she didn't want to disturb the dogs and set up a ruckus. Lately there hadn't been many of those sit-cross-legged-in-the-middle-of-the-bed-and-tell-secrets times. She missed them. She was going to miss them even more when she moved away in January.

Kitty nudged her sister. "I want every single detail and don't leave a thing out. *Everything,* Josie. By the way, why is Zip still here? I swear, you look positively iridescent."

"Paul asked me to marry him, Kitty."

Kitty clapped her hands. "And you said . . . what?"

"I said yes. Do you believe that, Kitty? I said yes. I didn't even think about it. Marie Lobelia is his mother. He found his niece and her little boy. I went with him. He gave up the family business and is now a partner with Jack Emery. He's . . . he's . . . wonderful. It's like he shed this skin that wasn't his and now the *real* Paul Brouillette is here. My God, I love that man! Mom approves. It's so weird. First it was the lilies of the valley and then it was the pearls and . . . I know she approves. Everything just suddenly fell into place. I couldn't want or ask for anything more. Is that how it was with you and Harry?"

"Yes, and it's still like that. I'm glad you didn't get upset when I called in for the extra day. It's nice to have reliable help to take up the slack. That was a good decision on our part to hire her. So, when's the wedding?"

"Paul wants it soon. I don't have a dress. I told him maybe August at the earliest. What I would really like is a double wedding with you and Harry. Can you switch up?"

"I might be able to twist Harry's arm. I'll have to cancel the hall and a bunch of stuff if we have it here in the garden. That's what you want, isn't it?"

Josie nodded. "If we do it here, Mom and Dad can come. Their spirits are here, Josie. I feel it. Mom always said the only thing she wanted was for the two of us to be happy. But, maybe once we get married, and she sees we're happy, she'll leave. Do you think that will happen?"

"I don't know, Josie, but you have to let it go. Mom's gone. Life goes on."

"I know that, Kitty. I know, too, that it's all wishful thinking on my part. My pearls broke because I pulled on them. The lilies of the valley are flowers and flowers give off a scent. Branches sway and leaves rustle because of a breeze that comes out of nowhere. I know all that. It just makes me feel better to *believe*. All I wanted was to say good-bye."

"Things will change now, Josie. You have Paul. You're going to get married, and you'll have kids and so will I. It will be our life like Mom had her life. We'll still have our memories even when we're old with gray hair. We have each other. That's never going to change. If it's any consolation to you, I felt exactly the same way until I met Harry."

"You never said a thing. Why?"

"I thought you'd laugh at me. Like you, it was wishful thinking on my part. I didn't get to say good-bye, either. There's a logical explanation for everything if you look hard enough to find it. We simply didn't want to look. I wanted to believe, too."

Josie felt her eyes mist over. "If ever we needed a sign, now is the time." Both girls grew quiet and looked around. Nothing happened. The fan overhead whirred softly. The refrigerator hummed the way it always did. Outside the birds chittered in the trees the same way they did every morning. The prevailing scent of the day was cinnamon from a plug-in deodorizer. She shrugged. Kitty smiled.

"Tell me about the niece, Josie."

"She's young, and her little boy is adorable, but he has a hearing problem. He knows how to sign. His mother taught him. It's sad, but I know Paul will do everything in his power to make it right for the child. They're staying at his house until he decides how he wants to handle it. At first he wanted to wait till Mother's Day, but I more or less talked him out of that. He wants what we all want from our parents—approval. He told me he played so many scenarios over and over in his mind about how he was going to walk into his mother's house with his niece and his great-nephew until he got dizzy. I hope he can come away happy. I hope Marie can convince him that she truly does love him. Why is it, Kitty, that people are so stubborn sometimes?"

Kitty grinned. "If I knew that, I'd write a book."

"What I don't want to see happen is what I think will happen. Paul's going to take Nancy and Pete to his mother, explain the situation, and turn around and leave. It's going to be one of those see, I did this for you even though you did all those terrible things to me. He doesn't understand what it is to grieve for the death of a child. He's afraid to open up where his mother is concerned. He won't run the risk of being hurt again. He's got that hurt all packaged neatly in the back of his mind and heart, and he isn't about to open it up."

Kitty propped her chin on her elbow and stared across the table at her sister. Her free hand traced the strawberry on the coffee cup. "Maybe you need to help things along a little."

"You mean interfere? I can't do that, Kitty."

"Then how about if I do it? I could go and talk to Marie and explain it all."

"This is none of our business. It's something Paul has to do on his own. He has to do what is right for him, what he can live with."

"A nudge then. Just a little one. We could go to Marie's together. I could bake a cream praline pie and we can take it with us. Let's do it, Josie. This is Sunday. Tomorrow or Tuesday he'll decide to take his niece and nephew over there. She's an old lady. Maybe the shock will do something to her."

"No. We aren't going to interfere. Paul has to find his own way."

"Then I guess there's nothing left to say. I have to get to work. Did you get that mint tea I asked you to pick up for the high tea we're serving this afternoon?"

"Two big boxes. They're on the kitchen counter."

Kitty waltzed over to the counter as she sang, off-key, the words to her newest favorite song . . . *"Now let me ask you quite honestly, do you know me or just like what you see? Wearin' dresses just above the knee, it might be pleasin' but it's killing me!"*

Josie chimed in, her arm around her sister's shoulders.

"I'm getting rid of all my pantyhose, and all those high heels with the pointy toes. I'm gonna find myself some comfortable clothes, and I'm getting rid of all my pantyhose."

"You better not quit your day job either." Kitty laughed. "I acted it all out for Harry. The song I mean. I combed my hair like Corinda Carford and really put on a show for him. By the way, what happened to the mangos?"

"I threw them out because they turned black and squishy," Josie said.

"A likely story."

"I didn't . . . I wouldn't . . . they were rotten! Kittyyyyy!"

Kitty was halfway down the path to the test kitchen when she called over her shoulder, "If you say so."

"I do say so," Josie muttered.

Paul sat in the waiting room, his niece's hand in his. He smiled reassuringly.

"What's taking so long? He's been in there for hours."

"I guess it's a delicate operation. Dr. Tumin is a fine pediatric surgeon. I'm sure Pete will come out of this just the way he said he would. He's going to be fine. Two days in the hospital, and he goes home. They've agreed to let you stay with him around the clock. I hired a private-duty nurse. We've got it covered. It's Ollie I'm worried about. He's never been away from Pete."

"Ollie will be fine. I gave him one of Pete's socks and an old shirt. He sleeps with them. As long as you walk him every four hours, he's fine. He knows Pete's coming back. He likes your house. There's lots of room for him to run around. It's hard for me to believe we've been here a whole month. When are we going to meet my grandmother? Have you given any thought to the fact that she might not welcome us with open arms?"

"I don't think there will be a problem. I thought it best to wait until Pete was over his surgery. There would be less strain on you and the boy. My mother, too, for that matter. My plan is to take you to the house on Sunday. Did your father ever tell you about the courtyard?"

"No."

"It's just perfect for a little boy to play in. It's all bricked with fountains and flowers and walls. Moss grows between the bricks. There's a magnificent old oak tree Pete will itch to climb as he gets a little older. It was my favorite place when I was little. Your mother and I used to climb it and scare the daylights out of our mother. She said we were agile as monkeys."

"What was my mother like?"

"She was so very pretty. She was kind. Sometimes siblings aren't kind to one another, but she was. She always had time for me. I imagine I was a bit of a pest back in those days."

"Was my father devastated when she died? Is that

why he turned out the way he is? Why did he take me away?"

"I can only guess and repeat the things I heard the grown-ups say. I don't know if it's true or not. Your father wasn't fond of working. My parents supported your mother and father for a long time. They didn't want their oldest daughter to lack for anything. Maybe they over-whelmed your father. Maybe he thought he wasn't good enough to belong to the family. But because your mother loved him, my parents made the best of it. Perhaps they shouldered too much of the burden. I simply don't know, Nancy. What I do know for a fact is your mother had a very healthy bank account, thanks to your grandparents. She had a lot of jewelry that he took along with the money. Jewelry that should go to you. I don't know if he sold it off or not. I do know he cleaned out the bank account. That's about all I can tell you."

"Tell me about my grandmother."

Here it was, the one thing he didn't want to talk about. How was he to tell this anxious mother he really didn't know his own mother? "You'll like her. She can be warm and witty. She never much cared for cooking or keeping house. My father indulged her and let her work in the cornmeal plant. She did a wonderful job but for some rea-son she was not up for change. She wanted to keep every-thing the way it was. It was almost as though she found herself caught up in a time warp. You see, things changed after your mother died, and then my other sister died. It was very hard on her. I'm sure she will dote on Pete. She's frail now, and she lives in the French Quarter—in our old house—with her sisters. They watch soap operas and play cards. You and Pete will be like a breath of fresh air for all of them. There's nothing for you to worry about on that score. The doctor's coming," Paul said, squeezing his niece's hands.

"The boy's fine. You can see him now if you like. He's not quite awake, but he did ask about Ollie. I assumed he was a pet, so I said he was sleeping. You might want to reassure him on that score. Pete will hear, in time—a month, possibly a little longer—just like any other little boy."

"Thank you so much," Nancy said tearfully as she clung to Paul's arm.

"If you follow me, I'll take you to Pete's room."

Paul stared through the glass at the little boy lying in the hospital bed, a nurse at his side. "I'll leave you two alone, Nancy. It's time to walk Ollie. I thought I would take a Polaroid shot of the dog and bring it back later. I have some meetings scheduled for this afternoon, but I'll stop on the way home from work. This evening I'll bring Josie by. I know she wants to see Pete."

Nancy stared at her son, only half-hearing her uncle's words. She nodded. It was all there in her face: the love she felt for her son, the worry, the anxiety, and the relief as well. And it was just an operation. What would she look like if the operation hadn't been successful or if something had gone awry and the boy had died on the operating table? She'd probably look the way his mother had looked the day June died. How well he remembered that awful blank, uncomprehending look and then the heart-wrenching scream that he still heard sometimes in his dreams.

"I need to say something besides thank you. Thank you just isn't enough."

"For me it is," Paul said lightly. "Do you want me to bring you anything? Food, magazines, anything at all?"

"No, thank you. I'll be fine. I can get some coffee later. Thank you for asking, though. I want to be the first person he sees when he wakes up."

"Of course. I'll see you around seven."

In the car on the way home, Paul dialed Josie's number. He wasn't surprised when she picked it up on the first ring. "He's okay, and he's going to hear just like every other kid. I can't tell you how relieved I am. Nancy was a wreck, but she's okay now. I'm on my way home to walk Ollie and then I have to get to the office. How about if I pick you up around six-thirty and we come on over here. It would be a big help if you walked Ollie. You did? What would I do without you, Josie? I love you so much my ears ache with the feeling." He listened to the delightful laugh on the other end of the line. "See you later."

When Josie woke on Sunday morning she thought it was just another Sunday until she remembered how important this particular day was to Paul. She literally flew out of bed, raced downstairs with the dogs, and let them out. She left the screen door open so they could let themselves in as she made coffee and then raced back upstairs to the shower. Paul was to pick her up at ten-thirty with Nancy, Pete, and Ollie. As she shampooed her hair, every scenario under the sun flashed in front of her. Would it work? Wouldn't it work? Would everyone make peace? Would things be all right? Would Marie Lobelia like the little boy or would he remind her too much of Paul? Would she welcome the young woman who looked so much like her own daughter or would she be aloof and withdrawn? Would Paul come away whole or would he have more burdens to carry away? She wished she knew and then again, she didn't want to know.

Josie was on her third cup of coffee when she heard Paul blow the horn in front of the house. They'd agreed to meet out front because of Zip and his reaction to the speckled dog. Kitty was watching them in the office; she'd agreed to stay with them until Josie returned home.

"Tell Miss Josie where you're going, Pete," Paul said, the moment Josie buckled up.

"Him's taking us to great-*grandmère's* house."

Josie laughed.

"He's so excited. So am I," Nancy bubbled. "Ollie is just shaking because he doesn't know what's going on."

"It's new to him. Wait till he sees that courtyard with the big tree. He can play out there all day with Pete. He's going to love it," Josie said.

"I called early this morning, but I guess everyone was at church. I didn't leave a message. It's okay. I have a key to the gate." Josie shivered at Paul's cool tone. She crossed her fingers, hoping everything would work out. She wondered what she would be feeling and how she would react if she were in Nancy's place. Plain and simple, she would be a basket case. How could anyone not love the adorable, dark-eyed little boy and his loving mother?

Ten minutes later, Paul parked his car at the curb. "Here we are, Pete. This is great-*grandmère's* house. Are you ready? Want to ride on my shoulders? I thought so. Climb on, sport. Josie, here's the key. Ring the bell and open the gate at the same time. I'm not playing any games here today."

Josie sucked in her breath but did as instructed. She shivered when she heard Paul shout, *"Mère,* it's Paul! I brought someone to see you." He stood still in the middle of the courtyard and waited. They all waited. Two minutes went by, then three, then four. He was about to shout a second time when the door to the kitchen opened.

Marie's voice was cool and aloof-sounding when she said, "It's customary to call ahead when bringing unexpected guests."

"Those are the old ways. Those ways don't apply anymore. I'd like to introduce you to your granddaughter Nancy and her son Pete. This four-legged creature is named Ollie. They all go together. That means they're a family. We can go out and come in again if you like."

Marie backed up a step and then another as she stared first at her son and then at her granddaughter and finally down to the little dark-haired boy. The dog barked a greeting, and she finally smiled. Her arms were trembling and shaking but she reached out, tears streaming down her cheeks.

Josie blinked when she saw that the outstretched arms

were for Paul, not Nancy and the little boy. She watched Paul's shoulders stiffen and then relax, a broad smile spreading across his face.

"You did this for me? One moment, chère," she said to Nancy. "This must come first. It has festered way too long. You have forgiven me?"

"I forgave you a long time ago, *Mère*. I just didn't know it until a few weeks ago."

Marie stared deeply into her son's eyes. Whatever she saw there reassured her. "We will speak of this at length later, my son. For now I want to feast my eyes on this beautiful young woman and her son."

Woof.

"And you, too." Marie smiled as she wrapped her arms around the shaking shoulders of her granddaughter.

Paul hoisted Pete to his shoulders. "This is your great-grandmother, Pete. Say hello."

"Hello, Great-*Grandmère*," the little boy said shyly.

"Come, come, we must go inside and talk. The aunts will want to meet you. They have much to talk about. I thought this day would never come. There are no words to tell you how happy I am this day. Chère, tell me, did you have something to do with all of this?" she asked Josie.

"*Mère,* Josie is my fiancée. I didn't know she knew you, and she didn't know I was your son. We're getting married the end of July."

"How wonderful! Such happiness I am having this day. I won't be able to sleep for weeks. I want to say something, but I don't know the words. My heart is so full. Come, come, let us go inside."

"I'll stay out here in the garden with Pete and Ollie. We'll be in in a little while," Paul said.

"You must tell the little one of your antics out here when you were his age. Your toys are in the shed behind the fountain. Bring them out for the boy."

"My toys! What toys?" Paul asked.

"Your wagon, your bicycle, your roller skates, your archery set. All your things."

"You saved them!" Paul said dumbfounded.

"But of course. Mothers do things like that. I have a lock of your hair in my locket. From your first hair trimming. You wailed like a banshee. Later we will compare it to little Pete's hair. I think it is the same color and texture. He looks like a Brouillette."

Josie burst out laughing at the stunned look on Paul's face.

"Paul. I'm going to go home now. This day is for you and your family. I want you to enjoy every single minute of it. I don't quite belong here yet. Please say you understand."

Paul smiled. "I understand, and you're right. I'll see you tomorrow."

"Her's nice," Pete said. "Are you going to kiss her?"

Paul dropped to his haunches. "Do you think I should?" he asked solemnly.

"Mommie said you give kisses when you love some one. My mommie kisses me all the time. She loves me."

"That's because you're easy to love, Pete. I think I'll do

what you suggested." In an exaggerated dip and swirl, Paul kissed Josie until her teeth rattled.

"Howzat?" he asked Pete. The little boy nodded happily.

"I'll see you tomorrow," Josie said, waving good-bye. "Paul . . ."

"Yes."

"Be open. Listen. You won't be sorry. Will you trust me on this?"

"Of course. I'll call you tonight."

"Only if you have time. I'm not going anywhere, and besides, I'm the type that will wait forever."

"That's good to know."

"You don't want to put it to the test, though." Josie laughed.

"You're right. I don't."

It was so quiet in the old house, which smelled of rich spices. Paul felt unnerved. It was time to talk to his mother, time to air all the hurts, time to make amends. How was he to do that in this quiet house? Should he whisper? Should he shout and carry on like a wild man? Or, should he just listen to his heart? In the end, the matter was taken out of his hands when his mother reached for his hand and drew him into the kitchen. She poured dark coffee laced with chicory just the way he liked it. He knew it would be rich, strong, and fragrant. For sure he wouldn't sleep for a week.

Marie leaned across the table. ''I think we both have

things we want to say. Perhaps this is the time, and perhaps it isn't. This estrangement all these years is my fault. Totally mine. I take full blame, full responsibility. An apology isn't good enough. Every day of my life I regretted my neglect of you. I couldn't help myself; therefore, I couldn't help you. It is that simple. When I finally got my wits together and joined the world, it was too late. You didn't want any part of me. It was hard for me to accept, but I did understand. For a while I tried to make your life miserable in retribution. It was the only way I could have contact with you. I don't care about the cornmeal plant. I never did, not really. It was something to keep me busy and something to fuss at you about. I just went through the motions. I was always a businesswoman, and I know about profit and loss. I was punishing you and myself for something I had no control over, or at least that's how I explained it to myself.

"I pray you and Josie never go through what I went through. There are no words to describe what it's like to lose a child. And then to lose a second child. It was so unthinkable, so tragic, I literally lost my mind. And I lost you in the bargain.

"What you did today was give me back my life. I can never thank you enough. Seeing Nancy and Pete took me back to those long-ago years. She looks exactly like June. She's warm and loving, and the little one is just like you were. God has blessed us both, Paul. They will be staying here with us. Pete is in your old room. Nancy is in her mother's room. Tomorrow we will all wake up and have breakfast together. Before you can ask, the dog is sleeping on Pete's bed. Such love, such devotion. One last thing. I never stopped loving you, son. That love was in my heart. I just ignored it, believing someday when I was ready, I could open it up like a book and go on and you would come running to me with open arms. That goes to show what a stupid old lady I was. Now that I'm even older, I'm more stupid because I am still hoping you can forgive me and love me as I love you."

Paul's throat closed tight. He fought for words, just the right words. *Listen*, Josie had said.

"It's all in the past. I forgave you a long time ago, *mère*. We can go forward now. Nancy and Pete will be part of our lives. One day, soon, I hope, Josie and I will have children. You aren't angry then that André is taking over the business?"

"Not in the least. He's the ideal man for the job. I'm happy you decided to follow your heart and do what you've always wanted to do. You have my blessing. Also, there is no need for you to purchase the plant. That is what you planned on doing, isn't it? That is so like you, Paul. Trust me, it isn't necessary. I provided well for all the employees years ago when I sensed this was coming. They will rest in the sun now, as I plan on doing. I want to show you something."

Paul watched as his mother reached under the starched collar of her high-necked dress to remove a heavy gold locket. She snapped it open. "See, this is your picture, and this is a lock of your hair. I have worn this from the day you were born. Now," she said, reaching into her pocket to withdraw a tissue. She spread it open on the table. "It is the little one's hair. I took a snippet when he fell asleep. I defy you to tell the difference. He is you all over again. Maybe, with your help, God's help, I can do it right this time."

Paul blinked. He really needed to get his eyes checked. Of late, they burned a lot. "*We* can do it, *mère*."

"We are a family again?"

"Yes, we are a family again. God, I feel good," Paul said thumping the table.

Marie thumped the table herself. "Not as good as I feel, son."

"Come, *mère*, I'll walk you to your room."

"I used to walk you to your room. Imagine that."

Paul smiled. "Yes, imagine that."

Josie sat at her little dressing table, staring at her reflection. Her sister watched her from the bed. "Today's the day, Kitty! Do you think Mom knows we're getting married?"

"I hope so." Kitty's voice was so wistful-sounding, Josie rushed over to her and put her arms around her shoulders.

"Maybe we should cry now and get it out of our systems. Our mascara will run later on."

"It's not right, Josie. There's supposed to be a mother of the bride. In our case, mother of the brides. Plural. We don't have anyone on our side. Our side of the church is going to be totally empty. The first three pews are always reserved for family. Our friends will be there, but it's not the same. It isn't fair."

"I know, Kitty, but there's nothing we can do about it. Mom would tell us to pull up our socks and go on. I wrote her a letter last night. I stuffed it in with all the others."

"I did, too. It's in my sock drawer. Mom always said I had the messiest drawers. She said they were worse than yours. We're going to be happy, aren't we, Josie?"

"Yes, we are. We'll visit often, and we'll call every day. I'll be your kids' godmother and you'll be my kids' god-mother. Harry and Paul get along wonderfully even though they only met recently. We're a family. We're smaller than Paul's or Harry's, but we're still a family. I bought you a wedding present. It's kind of special—you know, a sister-to-sister kind of present. It's for Harry, too, but mostly for you. Do you want me to get it? It's in the spare room."

Kitty dabbed at her eyes and nodded. Josie was back within minutes, holding a small basket. A tiny, silky head peered over the top. She held the basket out to her sister. "Her name is Soho. She's a Goldenray Yorkie. I bought her from Cher Hildebrand in Dayton, Ohio. I picked her up at the airport last night while you were out with Harry's parents. Tell me I didn't make a mistake. Please, Kitty, tell me you love that little dog. I thought you wouldn't miss me so much if you had a dog to remind you of me."

"God, Josie, what's not to love? Would you look at this face. She's beautiful. She's gorgeous. I love her already. Harry is going to flip when he sees her. He just loves dogs. Thank you, Josie. I feel better now. I really do."

"Good, that's all that matters. You never did tell me what Harry gave you as a wedding present. Show me!"

"Swear you won't laugh."

"I swear," Josie said. "Where is it?"

"In my room on the bed. Listen, his heart was in the right place, so remember that."

"It's a . . ."

"Chef's coat with five stars and a high top hat."

"It's wonderful. Jewelry is such a drag," Josie said. "What did Paul give you?"

"He said he left it on the back porch, so I guess it isn't jewelry either. I forgot to open it. Wait, I'll go get it. It's a big box, too. I have a feeling it's going to be as romantic as your coat and hat."

Kitty cuddled with the little dog until Josie, huffing and puffing, shoved a huge carton into her bedroom. "Wow! Maybe we should guess what it is before you open it. Anticipation and all that."

Josie reached for her manicure scissors and slit the tape holding the box together. "Oh, Kitty, look at this." Josie held up a dinner plate with a huge strawberry in the middle. "It's just like Mom's. Wait, wait, here's a note."

"Read it, read it. Hurry up. What's it say?" Kitty squealed.

My darling Josie,

I wanted to give you something special for your wedding gift. I'm sorry to say I don't have an original bone in my body. However, I saw the look on your face the day you served me a cup of coffee in your mother's cup. It took me a while, but I finally found someone who said they could replicate it. There is a service for eight in this box, and I have the remainder at my house. I took the liberty of ordering a set for Kitty also.

"He didn't!" Kitty squealed. "God, Josie, this looks exactly like Mom's dishes. This is so perfect I can't stand it. You know what, Josie? We did all right for ourselves. We really did."

"You can say that again. We have to put our gowns on. The limo will be here in fifteen minutes. You help me with mine, and I'll help you with yours. Where's your veil?"

"I'm not wearing one. I'm wearing my chef's hat."

"No kidding! That takes guts!"

"I'm not carrying that dumb bouquet either."

"I'm almost afraid to ask, but what *are* you going to carry?"

"I wasn't going to carry anything till you gave me this dog. Now I'm going to carry her. Don't say it, Josie. This is my wedding, and you know what? It isn't as dumb as you might think. Mom wore a red garter you could see through her dress and her shoes were red. Dad loved it."

"I wasn't going to say a word. I think you should do whatever the hell you want to do. You're right. This is your wedding, too. I love you, Kitty."

"You won't be embarrassed?"

"Never."

"What about Paul?"

"He won't be embarrassed either. He's so laid-back

these days it's hard to believe he's the same guy. Okay, help me with my dress."

"My pleasure." Kitty grinned.

An hour later, Father Sebro said, "I now pronounce you man and wife. You may now kiss the bride!"

Paul turned, his gaze straying to the three empty pews on the right side of the church. A smile tugged at the corners of his mouth. He gently turned Josie's head. A smile that rivaled the sun spread across his new wife's face. All he was able to see was a flash of pink as the heady scent of lilies of the valley wafted toward him.

Kitty Dupré's Favorite Recipes

❧ ❧ ❧

❧ Fried Frog Legs ❧

12 pair frog legs
1 tsp cayenne pepper
2 tsp salt
2 eggs, beaten
1 c flour
¼ c cornmeal
1 tsp chili powder
fat for frying

Season frog legs with cayenne pepper and salt. Dip frog legs in egg, then roll in combined mixture of flour, cornmeal and chili powder. Fry in deep fat at 350°F for about 8 minutes or until golden brown and tender.

SERVES 4.

☘ Pepper Apple Chicken ☘

6 boneless chicken breasts
2 c apple juice
2 tbsp butter
2 large apples (I prefer Granny Smith)
1 tbsp black pepper
½ c brown sugar
1 tbsp ground cinnamon
¼ tbsp of nutmeg
1 tbsp cornstarch
¼ c water

Wash chicken and dry thoroughly. Allow chicken to soak in apple juice for two hours in refrigerator. Remove chicken from apple juice (save juice). In a skillet, melt butter. Add chicken, reduce heat from high to medium. Peel and core apples, slice as thin as possible. Turn chicken once after browned; then add apple slices. Spread evenly. Cover and allow to simmer until other side is browned. Add apple juice, nutmeg, brown sugar, cinnamon and pepper. Stir thoroughly and cover. Simmer 20–25 minutes. Mix cornstarch in water. When mixture starts to bubble, add cornstarch. Stir until thick. Serve hot.

❖ Corn Puppies* ❖

1½ c all-purpose flour
2 c corn flour or cornmeal
¼ tsp baking powder
¼ c sugar
¼ lb butter, melted
¾ c milk
2 large eggs
1 15 oz can whole kernel corn, 303 size can
4 c oil for frying
¼ to ½ c powdered sugar

In a mixing bowl combine all-purpose flour, corn flour (or cornmeal), baking powder and sugar. Blend with a mixer on medium high speed until totally blended. Continue to mix while you add all butter a little at a time until all is added. Continue to blend until pea-sized balls are formed. Slowly add milk to mixture while mixing on high speed. After all milk is added, add both eggs and blend until creamy thick texture. (**Note:** Mixture should be firm). Open can of corn and drain completely. Add corn to mixture and fold until evenly mixed.

Next, in a 1½ quart pot, heat oil to 300°F. Carefully spoon 2–3 tbsp of mixture into hot oil. As puppies begin to brown turn over a couple of times until evenly browned all over. Remove and drain on paper towels. To serve, place in a bowl and sprinkle powdered sugar on top by putting sugar into a wire strainer and tapping it with your hand while moving strainer all around the bowl to get even distribution of sugar.

SERVES 6–8.

❧ Jambalaya ❧

1 fryer, cut into pieces
1½ lb smoked hot sausage
3 tbsp shortening or bacon drippings
3 tbsp flour
2 medium onions, chopped
1 green pepper, chopped
2 cloves garlic, minced
2 c water
2 c canned stewing tomatoes
2 tbsp parsley, minced
¼ c green onion tops
2 tsp salt
2 c rice

Brown sausage and chicken in shortening or bacon drippings; remove, and add flour to make roux. Add onions, green pepper and garlic. Cook until tender. Add water, rice, tomatoes, parsley, onion tops, and salt. Stir in browned sausage and chicken. Bring to boil. Reduce heat to low temperature and cook covered for 1 hour.

SERVES 8–10.

❧ Shrimp Boulettes* ❧

¼ *c celery*
1 *c onions, chopped*
¼ *c green onions*
1 *c shrimp*
2 *eggs*
1 *c flour*
1 *c seasoned bread crumbs*
1 *tsp salt*
1 *tsp pepper*
2 *c oil for frying*

Grind celery, onions and green onions in a food processor. Drain excess liquid; then empty mixture into a mixing bowl. Grind raw peeled minced shrimp in a food processor. Add to mixture and blend. Add eggs (scrambled) and blend completely.

Add flour and bread crumbs to mixture until you achieve a thick pasty consistency. Add salt and pepper and mix. Heat oil to hot. Spoon tablespoon-sized balls into hot oil and cook until browned. Serve.

❖ Crawfish Étouffée ❖

2½ lb crawfish tails
1 stick margarine
3 large onions, finely chopped
finely chopped parsley
salt and pepper to taste

Sauté onions in margarine, about 15–20 minutes, until soft. Add crawfish fat and cook over low heat, stirring constantly, until fat comes to the top. Add tails and season to taste. Add just enough hot water to étouffée for desired consistency. Simmer for 20 minutes. Add parsley. Serve over steaming hot rice.

⚜ Cajun Crab Pie* ⚜

1 c onion, chopped
1½ c green onion, chopped
¼ c bell pepper, chopped
1 tbsp garlic, minced
3 tbsp butter
1 lb lump crabmeat
2 tsp salt
1 tsp cayenne pepper
2 tsp black pepper
1 lb cheddar cheese, shredded
3 tbsp lemon juice

⚜ The Crust ⚜

1 c self-rising flour
1 tbsp dry milk
1 tsp sugar
1 tsp salt
¼ tsp baking soda
1 c milk
3 eggs
1 tbsp butter

Preheat oven to 350°F. In a skillet, sauté onion, green onion, bell pepper and garlic in 3 tbsp butter until onion is clear. Remove from heat and add crabmeat, salt and both peppers (cayenne and black). In a separate bowl, combine flour, dry milk, sugar, salt, baking soda, milk, eggs and 1 tbsp butter and blend until smooth. Pour into greased 9″ x 12″ baking pan. Top with prepared crab mixture. Cover with shredded cheese and sprinkle on lemon juice. Bake covered for 35 minutes at 350°F. Uncover and bake at 400°F until brown.

SERVES 6–8.

Note: Be sure to clean crabmeat of all shell.

*with thanks to Chef Remy's *Dat Little Cajun Cookbook*. Write to Chef Remy at: *datcook@bellsouth.net*.

Fern Michaels likes to hear from her readers. Write to her c/o Kensington Publishing Corp. or E-mail her at:

fernmic@aol.com

* * *

Don't miss Fern Michaels's next paperback

THE GUEST LIST

(coming from Zebra Books in August 2000)

or her next hardcover

WHAT YOU WISH FOR

(coming from Kensington Publishing Corp. in October 2000)